CONTENTS

SEA LION SCENARIO

(David Nivens-unsplash)

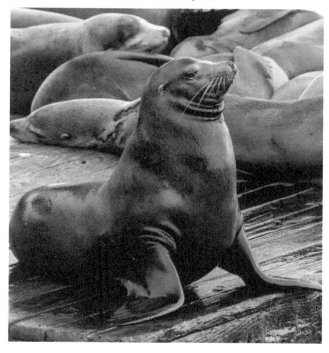

COPYRIGHT 2022

ASTORIA MYSTERIES
Sealion Scenario

By DeLores May Richards

PO Box 334 Astoria Or, 97103

ISBN: 9798768807993

ACKNOWLEDGEMENTS

THANKS TO THE SILVER SALMON GRILL,
FULIO'S AND TO THE ROGUE ALE HOUSE
AND FREE MUSEUM, THE LABOR TEMPLE
AND T PAUL'S SUPPER CLUB. A SPECIAL
THANKS TO THE ASTORIA POLICE FORCE
AND THE COAST GUARD FOR THEIR
EXCELLENT WORK.

COVER PHOTO BY DAVID
NIVENS(UPSPLASH)

DELORES MAY RICHARDS

Sea Lions here and Sea Lions there

At the East Mooring basin, they're everywhere.

It's not their neighborhood, certainly not their town.

They are still in the Columbia on docks all around.

They eat our fish; they chase all our boats and then they weigh down our docks and our floats.

From California they come. You see them every spring and when they come back their children they bring.

I'm tired of losing my fish off my pole. It's a story that hits me down deep in my soul.

Please California, come get your huge herd.

We'll help you ship them out. Just say the word.

CHAPTER 1: UPPERTOWN

AUTHOR: Coming into Astoria from the east, the first thing we see as we approach is the remarkable Columbia River. It flows today smooth and glass-like. Hardly a ripple is seen in this mid-September cloudless day. 68 degrees has been the preferred temperature for this small community. It attracts tourists from the greater Portland area in droves. A writer is always looking for new stories and with the conviction of the 'Killer Clown,' we see a city packed full of interested out-of-town individuals. We are here to document the verdict for our last book. But this was a surprise. I like Astoria. It comes at you like a blast of fresh air. However, this blast of fresh air is filled with a new mystery. Barely had the verdict came into the station about the conviction of the 'The Clown'(first book in this series) when CSI O'Neal—preparing to head home for the evening—received a telephone call. It was a body! He nodded at Officer George and said, "We've got another body—in the river."

So, as we come into the city, on the right, I note the Rogue Ales Public House with a long approach on a wooden piling street. It is located at pier thirty-nine. It opened in 2007 and now serves—not only as a restaurant and Ale house—but also as a free museum. It honors the old Bumblebee cannery and has historic value in the equipment it keeps within its walls.

We will be coming back to this restaurant. (please see the pages at the end of this book.) We will be looking at the old Astoria Railroad and the Trolley.

The Rouge Ales Public House and museum seen from the highway

You may ask "When I speak about us, who is that extra person?" I see your concern. Writers often say 'we.' The reason I am saying 'we' however, is that I have another person in my little white Pirus. You want to know who that is? It's YOU, dear reader, and you and I are going to help solve this crime together. So, fasten your seat belt and 'LET'S GO!' Three blocks down, we see the California Sea Lions which migrate every year to Astoria by the hundreds. They are weighing down the docks and barking like your most irritated dogs. They are in unison—like one voice--always expressing their delight or their annoyance for what they receive from the world at large. That's where we want to go. The long causeway road is now closed to car traffic and foot traffic for safety reasons. The causeway was built after World War II. No longer could the public use it in 2018. It now has three police cars parked at its gate. The Sea Lions are barking.

Lights are flashing and other cars have pulled into the public parking area to catch a glimpse from afar. There is no way we can even get into that parking lot. It is a disaster.

Our reports to you will be concentrated on what happened. These facts—or rumors, you might say—comes to us by those nearby.

Uppertown-Here we come!

Sea Lions on the dock in Astoria from a distance

CHAPTER 2 MURDER AND LIONS

It seems that a young couple taking an evening run on the almost 13-mile Riverwalk—a Juliet and Perry Frazee— got tired and stopped to look over at the Sea Lions. They were both out of breath. They sat down on the bank together and sighted something strange lying in the water. It was in vast contrast to the gray and brown color of the Sea Lions on the pier. What was it? " Do you see those colors there in the water?" Juliet said. "Seems so out of place. What did the Sea Lions drag in now? They are such pests!"
Perry looked where she was pointing. " I see something also! Do you have your binoculars with you?"

"I do." She pulled off her backpack, searched through, and produced a small pair. She handed them to Perry. He focused them on the scene quite intently.

"It looks like a person floating out there—a woman! Yes—I believe-- a woman. She's got on a bright green dress or blouse. It's hard to see from this distance. We better call 911."

He pulled out his phone while Juliet took the glasses from him to see what her husband had seen. She was shocked!

Cragen O'Neal, George and the other officers got

there quickly. The police station was only 6 blocks away. It was late afternoon, September 17th, 2021.

Sea Lions in the Pacific Northwest

(Photo by Kristen Jarvis)

After borrowing their binoculars, CSI Cragen O'Neal said "George, call Nick and have him bring a boat in." And then to the helpful couple, "Thank you, folks. You've got very sharp eyes. That is hard to see from this distance. Leave your names with my officers. I'll contact you if we need to."

Then they opened the gate and moved at a fast

pace to get a better view. There must be at least one hundred Sea Lions lolling about in the late afternoon sun—about a third of them weigh 800 TO 1000 pounds. We can see them from here. It seemed like the officers could almost reach out and touch them. How are they possibly going to get this body out of these waters?

CSI O'Neal thought to himself 'She's still alive.' He started to place a leg over the rail. O'Neal pushed a lock of red hair out of his eyes and was going to jump in, but Officer George pulled him aside. "No, sir, I can see from here, she's not alive. Note her color and there is no movement whatsoever. Let's wait for the boat."

"George, you know this city. I have been here a very short time. What's with these critters?"

George had been studying Astoria all his life and he was instrumental in bringing the 'Killer Clown' to justice. He knew the city. He knew the history. His 6 ft 2 height towered over most men. It was quite noticeable when he stretched up tall as he did now. He was proud of the fact that the boss counted on him so much for these details. He looked over the guard rail. "Well, these guys migrate from California every year. They have not gone back yet. They eat the salmon and destroy the docks. They are terrible. Sea Lions this big, although they are peaceful mammals, can be dangerous if provoked. The city of Astoria has tried to get rid of their Sea Lions in non-lethal manners. The Lions are protected by law. They have tried balloons, fencing wire, and air dancers like they have at car dealers. A motorized fiberglass fake Orca failed big time. Poor Orca was a loser. You should have seen that. I laughed so much I was crying!"

"This is a dilemma for us, isn't it?"

George 's answer turned serious, "Yes, it is."

"Can we shoot a gun off to scare them away temporarily?" Cragen O'Neal took another look at the dock they were resting on. "I don't see how they are not breaking that dock down. They are heavy!"

"They are sir. And if we scare them, there is a good chance that body will disappear. We'll have a tough time finding it."

"Looks like a lady with a long green gown—red headed, tall. Have we had any reports of missing women, George?"

"None whatsoever, sir."

" I know we are tired. The 'Killer Clown' case was a doozy. I think we both put overtime in on that one."

" We did! We did!"

George and Cragen are waiting for a Coast Guard boat, and they have an interesting scenario. So, let's walk in a little closer. We can see them shrugging their shoulders in despair. They are watching the lady in the green dress as she floats within reach of the Sea Lions. What happens if they get excited and start moving around more? Right now, since they have hundreds of tourists coming to view them, they are not getting annoyed even with the police cars and their red lights flashing. Just another day in the life of a sea lion--barking away.

The Coast Guard boat comes in. Officer Nick has them get as close as they can. They are within talking distance of George and Cragen. The officers lean over the rail.

Knowing the coast guard solves all kinds of Ocean and River problems, Officer George directed his question to Petty Officer Lewis Jordon. He knew him well. "What are we going to do, Lewis?"

He answered with authority "We just cannot pull her out of these waters. It not only endangers us but also we could lose the body."

"Do you have any suggestions?" CSI Cragen asked.

"Knowing these lions, I suspect that they might be encouraged to leave if we could get another boat in here with scraps from the canneries. It should be the right time of day for leftovers to be available. We will go find a fishing boat and see if we can put something together. Sea Lions are quite used to following fishing boats and stealing what fish they can. We'll have to lure them down the river. They also know the sound of a fishing boat. So, when they see and hear the boat, they will be right on it. The boat can then drop part of their load and coax the Lions away. You'll have enough time to get the body out. However, It will take us a bit. We'll get started now."

The Coast Guard boat pulled out and headed west towards the canneries.

CHAPTER 3 OUR COAST GUARD

While we are waiting, let's go over details about our local Coast Guard. The area from Tillamook, Oregon to Vancouver Island is called the 'Graveyard of the Pacific.' The Coast Guard has a history of saving lives on the Columbia River. The Columbia River Bar is one of the most treacherous places to be in the world. Even though we see rescues, an experienced fisherman can be lost. The Coast Guard is always ready to go out when help is needed. Two thousand ships have been lost--700 lives at the Columbia River Bar alone. The Coast Guard has as its base at Tongue Point in East Astoria. It also has a helicopter base at the Astoria- Warrenton airport which was established in 1964.

Each year we read about another lost life or fishing boat in our daily paper. Many have been good acquaintances. The coast guard continually rescues tourists who do not realize the ocean's dangers. Fisherman who are experienced and still get trapped by the amazing five-minute change in weather conditions are sometimes lost.

They locate lost persons; they serve our area, and we extend thanks to them for their work. Occasionally, they lose numbers of their own in trying to save others.

And, let me tell you about something I have researched on the net! The Coast Guard ship 'Steadfast' calls Astoria its home. You can see it close to the Astoria Museum if it is in.

Commissioned in 1968. It spent its first 24 years in Florida. In 1994, its home became Astoria Oregon. It patrols the entire region down into central America.

There are so many news stories about their work-tracking drugs and migrant smuggling along the western seaboard and the coast of central America. I can hardly list them all.

Here are only a couple of their successes:

Oct 2020-- 67 million dollars' worth of cocaine from five smuggling vessels-almost four thousand pounds of cocaine.

May 2021-- 33 Million dollars' worth of Cocaine: a 49-day, 10,000-mile trip. (2400 pounds)

Words fail us. We can only say thanks!

THE STEADFAST DOCKED IN ASTORIA
(Public domain Wikipedia-- author Sandel)

The US Coast Guard ship in the Columbia River

Sits right across from the museum's history.

It sits there when it has no cargo to deliver

It becomes to us quite ordinary.

But it's not. No, it's not. It's merely on furlough.

You can find it there for days on end
and its activity is slow.

But all at once you hear the engine.
All at once you see the crew.

They are off to ocean parts to collect up
illegal cocaine---and that ship's crew!

CHAPTER 4   SEA LION LADY

It took a half hour for Officer Nick and Petty Officer Jordan to return followed by the fishing boat as a Sea Lion lure. We could see their crew tossing fish scraps from the boat out in the middle of the river and we could see the immediate reaction of hungry Sea Lions as they slid into the Columbia and headed to the boat. The boat pulled away. The Lions followed. The rescue boat was able to slide in close enough to the dock for a couple of officers to load the body onboard. It didn't take long with a clear dock. The Sea Lions had not disturbed the body.

"Careful there, guys. Let's give this lady respect as we bring her in!"

They were careful.

The crowd standing on the riverbank was quick to disperse after the boat left and we also left to await what the police were finding out about the 'Sea Lion Lady.'

We heard that she was taken off the boat to the morgue in a police van.

Dr Summers arrived at the morgue. He had two weeks to go to retirement. This would be his last patient. She was beautiful and young—in her thirties. Such a shame! He looked down at her, his tired old eyes taking in her every feature. She had dyed her hair red. He had closed the lids on her blue eyes. The lipstick had washed off her face except for a touch of orange. Her body had not been abused by drugs or alcohol. He could usually tell. Her body was firm, and he could see that she had walked to keep herself in perfect shape. The legs showed the muscles were well coordinated. Her hands looked like her fingers were creased with callouses. He suspected that she was a guitar player who was used to playing every day. Was she a professional musician?

Who was she? There was no purse or pocket to carry ID. Where did she come from? And how did she end up in the water? There was a large swelling on her head, but no signs of any other injury. She had been dead for close to about 18 hours. It was hard to tell.

"Well, what do you see, Doctor?" O'Neal was at his side.

" She's a very pretty, healthy girl. I say a day and a half in the water—not much more. She either accidently drowned or was hit on the head and ended up in the water. Her lungs show definitely signs of water. Cause of death was drowning. Do you have any reports of missing women?"

"None so far. We'll give her description to the Daily Astorian. Someone will call in." Cragen O'Neal shook his head in disbelief.

" She was also probably a musician. Her fingers were quite calloused."

Cragen O'Neal nodded.

"That's interesting to know. I'm heading back to the office."

He opened the morgue door. He paused as Dr Summers said "I'll have the report there in about an hour.

"Thanks, John." In the office, he called George in and gave him the girl's description for the newspaper. George wrote it all down. Anything else would have to wait for tomorrow. George was to meet his fiancée, Mary Bell for supper at T. Paul's Supper Club at 7:00. Time was passing quickly. He called the paper, said goodnight and headed in that direction.

Mary was sitting at their table with her back towards him. George could see her beautiful blond hair which had a slight curl. She turned, saw George, stood up and stretched up from her 5-foot statue and greeted him with a kiss on the cheek. " Hi, Hon. How was your day?" she said.

He laid his mask aside and returned the peck on the check and said, " I thought we were through with murder, but we got a call this afternoon-- just as we started home for the weekend. There was a body down at the dock floating in the water, right where the Sea Lions are."

Mary gasped. "Oh, no! Who was it?"

" Very pretty lady—no ID—nothing. Looks like she either hit her head and fell in or she was attacked and thrown in the water. It's too soon to know. She could have been a professional musician—maybe a guitar player. The staff is on it, and we may know more tomorrow. No one recognized her. She may not be local. How are you doing tonight?"

"I've been thinking of all the blessings I've received these past few months. I'm so relieved that the verdict in the clown case came in ok. I was dreading that the clown would not be convicted. Then I would have been returned to the list of suspects! I've had so many mixed emotions. It has freed my mind and I can go on with life."

"Yes, that was a worry for me too. I have grown to love you, Mary. I want you to know that."

Mary smiled. Her blue eyes always sparkled when she talked to George. "I'm serious about moving on with my life—no more bar jobs. I'm ready to get on ahead in a better way. I've noted, you have an opening coming at the office for dispatch. You think I could apply?"

"We are about six persons short. I'm sure you can get on. I would love to have you there in the office."

" OK, I'll be down there tomorrow—first thing."

The waiter came by and gave the specials.   T. Paul's had moved in 2009 to this terrific location across from the Hotel Elliot and right there by the Liberty theater. The food was good. Their business was good. They were on limited hours because of Covid-19 regulations which were back in full force. There was a lone musician presenting the entertainment for the evening. They ordered. George had Tenderloin steak and Mary, Fettuccine Alfredo. Since George had been so busy with overtime at work, they took this brief time to catch up on their lives. George walked Mary to her apartment, and they parted.

CHAPTER 6 IDENTIFYING THE REDHEAD

We wondered who the deceased lady was. We talked it over. We saw the description come out on the on-line newspaper site and we waited. It didn't take long. When Officer George Van and CSI O'Neal got into the office the next day, there was a message waiting for them. It was from the captain of a riverboat cruise. He owned a boat that had just started cruises up the Columbia River from Portland. He named his boat 'My Bonnie.' They had hired a traditional Scotch-Irish band to play a number of times a day. They were popular. He reported that the beautiful red-headed Irish girl that sang for them was missing on their last trip back.

This morning, they would be going back to Portland, but they always give their guests a couple of hours to see Astoria.

Cragen O'Neal and George were of one mind. They both headed to a car!

" Are you with me on this case too, George.? I'll need all the help I can get!

" I'm with you, sir!"

My Bonnie was a good-sized boat. She was only 250 feet long. She could carry about 100 guests and the crew. Being one of the few doing river cruises during the pandemic, she was usually fully booked. Guests were on both decks.

The captain was there to greet them. He introduced himself as Captain Finnian Murphy. He had been working on cruise ships for ten years. He was not a captain before, however. He was part of the ship's crew. When the pandemic shut down the cruise ships, he decided to buy his own boat and run it. His dark hair had graying at the temples which showed that he had certainly been around for a while. He was handsome—had a wife and children at home.

"I'm CSI O'Neal and this is Officer George Van. Thank you for calling. What can you tell us?"

Captain Murphy wrinkled his brow. "I hired these kids because I saw them in a Portland restaurant playing Irish music. They were popular. I pay them good, and they add just the right touch to our tour. They haven't failed me. Some take our cruise just for the music."

" How many of them are there?"

"Four now. We have a stage on this floor and 'My Bonnie' had been built so there is an opportunity to look over the edge of the top deck to see the band. We also have a closed-circuit TV inside where guests can watch if they don't want to be out in the air."

O'Neal identified with the captain, being Irish himself. He pushed his red hair off his brow and said, "Do you keep copies of the viewings?"

"Yes, we do. Most of the boat has cameras. I can send

the password with you if you like. They're on the net."

"I think it would help us. We are going to want to see what the band is like—whether they had disagreements and so forth. What was the deceased's name and where was she from?"

"She was a very beautiful lady. If I weren't married, you can bet I would be wanting her for a sweetheart." The captain was quick to answer. "Quinn Gallagher was her name-and she was from Beaverton, Oregon. It's part of Portland actually."

"I've been to Beaverton often, sir." Said George. It's quite the shopping and medical center. And it's easy getting to it on Highway 26 out of Seaside." George turned and looked at the boat. " This is a nice boat, Captain."

"Actually, I was on unemployment for a while. This boat came up for sale. I discovered there was money to help people out of this recession. They financed it for me. I'm certainly happy with the way it's going. It is bringing in the money and paying the bills. And being mostly outside, we can stay apart and avoid masks. I'm hoping we can run the season pretty late. Sometimes people like a stormy trip also. So that is good!"

O'Neal questioned the captain." Is the band here?"

"Yes, they are gathered upstairs in their dressing room." He led the way.

Cragen O'Neal said, "Since she was on the boat, we have to consider that something happened here. Can we have our force search your ship? I can have them here quick."

"No problem. I want to help. "Captain Murphy stated.

" We won't keep you long. George, call the office. Get about three or four guys here and we'll get this done fast."

Yes, sir." George pulled out his cell phone and turned away.

(Quinn Gallagher admiring the Columbia River she loved on the 'My Bonnie' riverboat cruise)   adobe stock 234361306

CHAPTER 7 THE BAND:

The four remaining members of the band were gathered together. All were wearing green. The bass player-- the only other girl in the band-- had a full-length gown almost identical to Quinn Gallagher's. Her name was Maddie McDowell. She was married to the band leader, Rory McDowell. The two of them had met in their native Ireland and married. Rory played violin. They were both talented in old Celtic jigs and folk songs. To Rory's right was a younger man, Danny Malone and he was conversing with another member, Adam Reilly, the Mandolin player. Danny Malone played the Banjo and sometimes did special numbers on the Irish Bouzouki. George, being a banjo player, was impressed with the appearance of the band. Some bands are not eager to have a banjo. Rory greeted both officers and they sat down at a table which held all their coffee cups. He poured both of them a cup and then everyone introduced themselves.

Quinn had not come back from yesterday's layover. She had left by herself at 5:00 PM and no one had seen her since. She seemed a little ill at ease and didn't want to be with the band on break. Had she ever did this before? Never, of course! Had they noted anyone with her at any time? Maddie spoke up. "I know it was unusual that she left by herself. Usually, we all go off together and find something to do during that time. Sometimes we split up but usually not. She was heading for the downtown area alone."

Adam said, " She didn't know anyone in Astoria. Myself-- I adored her. But we were just friends. She didn't seem to want to be close to anyone. I must say I did try. I asked her over and over for a date-- wasn't in the cards. Didn't have a beau either. Sure look! You dig? Don'tna. She never talked much about her life. We are a close group here—always sharing. She didn't. It was just singing with her. That's where her heart was. She was a terrific lead singer. It was like her guitar and her voice were joined together in some kind of a union. Those blue eyes would flash, and her red hair would bounce. She would play to the audience. That was her love! She was a 'Beour' fa sure. Adam let his Irish heritage show up in his brogue and expressions.

Rory shook his head. " We are going to miss her, I know. I need to find someone to fill this missing spot immediately. Quinn was a spring addition to our band. We don't know a whole lot about her history. She was formerly on an ocean cruise liner and Captain Murphy remembered her and asked us to hire her. I must say she has been wonderful. He certainly did not make a mistake."

" I know someone that could fill in for you. She's unemployed for a few weeks. She's a singer-song writer. I have heard her do Irish music. Do you want me to call her?" George was thinking about his perfect Mary, the love of his life.

"Would you do that? Can she come immediately so I can hear her? The show this morning seemed so incomplete without Quinn."

" I'll step out now and give her a ring." He opened the door and left. CSI Cragen continued to question the band.

Mary answered immediately as George stood at the rail looking out over the river.

"Yes, Hon?"

"This lady was a main part of their show. They need an extra singer immediately. Can you grab your guitar and come over?"

"Really? I'd love that! I applied for dispatcher. Looks like I might get it, but I'm at loose ends for a time. I can do it!"

" Might help to keep an eye on this band till we get it sorted out, too. You could be an immense help to the force. They leave in about an hour. You'll have to scoot right over. They want you for the show back —try out. Of course." (Mary Bell with her tenor guitar)

(Adobe Stock 234361305)

"Wow! She's a short one, Rory stated when he saw her."

" I doubt she's five feet, but dynamite in that little package. Please take good care of her!" George said.

Mary went to the stage, tuned her tenor guitar and started singing an Irish tune—'Molly Malone'—in an Irish brogue.

"Dang! This girl's good." Rory listened intently for a moment and motioned her down from the stage.

George told her goodbye and cautioned her to be on guard and left. She was as close as his phone. That weekend, Mary called George and told him she was ok. It was an excellent job and fun. They had a cot in the dressing room for her to sleep on. She would be spending nights there so she could learn their songs. She would be home on Tuesday night, however. She could miss one evening and morning show. She needed fresh clothes and her own bed. She was paying attention to what the band said—especially about Quinn. She sent him a video on her phone.

CHAPTER 8 TROUBLE AT THE DOCKS

(TUESDAY SEPTEMBER 21ST)

It was the following Tuesday afternoon. My guest and I had just finished eating at the Rogue Ale Public House and we were walking out the door to my car when I heard a loud sound coming from the Sea Lion dock. "What was that?" I said.

I looked down the street at the dock. I could see the wood and metal moving and it had a weird sound to it. We quickly walked down to the dock gate. Part of the causeway had definitely collapsed into the river with the electrical system for the boats. It was a Northern section, and it could be seen from the gate —but just barely.

The East Mooring Base in Upperton had been constructed right after World War II and the dock has been closed since 2018 because of rot. Lack of funds had prevented even a repair to the causeway. The material that fell into the water could do damage to docks and to boats.

I was amazed that this didn't happen when they were there last week. The officers were on the causeway. That would have been a disaster!

The police were already there—being less than a half-dozen short blocks away. They were there within five minutes. And they were putting up more barriers and seeing to the needs of the boats.

Days later I read in the Astorian where Bergersen Construction had been given a contract for $100,000 to remove the debris. It was a big job. At that time, and even a couple of days after the failure, equipment was already in place. The Port is looking for a state grant to rehab the causeway.

21

HERE WE ARE! 65 YEARS

CHAPTER 9 THE 65TH ANNIVERSARY (SEPTEMBER 24)

An author deserves a break from writing when it comes to special occasions. And despite all the writing I have done, I have to take this special day to celebrate. An An author deserves a break and despite all the writing I have done, I have to take this special day to celebrate with 'the love of my life!' So, I will break here for that. My special crime-solving passenger will have to find her way alone today.

There is no special celebration in order at this time because of Covid-19. No long trips have been planned. But today we are 'alone together.' When the kids are grown, when the grandkids have arrived on the scene, and a great grandchild or two also, it is important to take time to celebrate a very special date by yourselves.

And so, we did! I closed the computer down and the camera, and the note-taking was no longer in review. We made a reservation at one of our favorite restaurants in Astoria. It's the Silver Salmon Grill on Commercial street. It now includes 'New Orleans' style dishes. Those dishes are the work of a chef, who after experiencing the New Orleans scene and New York, owned Lil' Bayou in Seaside—John Sowa. Yes, we certainly remember the tasty food there!

This building is another of Astoria's historic gems.

The Fisher Building was designed and built in 1924 by John E Wicks. He designed a number of the buildings downtown as Astoria rebuilt after the 1922 fire.

The Thiel Brother's restaurant was in existence for 50 years and after a few exchanges of ownership, Jeff and Laurie Martin took over the building in 2001 and remodeled to suit their needs.

And I see you are looking at that very special bar. 1880's—made of Scottish Cherry wood which was placed in this location. It has quite a history. Formerly it was used in a house of ill repute, lost at the Port of Astoria in the 1920's and finally refurbished in and installed in this building in the fifties.

Ken and I still smiling after 65 years

CHAPTER 10 REVIEW AT THE OFFICE: (SEPTEMBER 28TH)

Although they had been putting together the autopsy, the research, and the crime scene investigation, things were slow in coming together for the Department. The past few days were being reviewed in Cragen O'Neal's office. Coffee cups in hand and paperwork folded on the table, everyone was on alert for further instructions.

O'Neal's first order of business was always to ask what his team had discovered, and he was doing just that. "Dr Summers, would you go over what you found in your examination? Don't skip over anything!"

"Definitely drowning! There was a severe bump on her head—but it wouldn't have killed her. We have been trying to determine how she hit her head or if something was used to do that to her. It was an unusual bump impression. I'm still trying to decide what that is. It's hard to tell whether this one is an accident or murder She had dinner right before her death and it was Italian food of some sort. There was wine, but not in excess. Death came shortly after that. I found no poisoning either. She was in perfect health—a very beautiful lady." He shrugged his shoulders.

" Was she molested?"

"No," he said. "Not any sign of that."

Cragen raised his voice. "George, here's something for you to research. We have an Italian restaurant on Commercial Street. See if you can find out anything. Who was she with and when they were there? Also check other town restaurants if you have no results there. More than one would have an Italian dish of some kind."

Dr Summers elaborated. "Spaghetti." He leaned back in his chair.

"Possibly Chicken Parmesan." he added.

"Yes sir, I'll start that this afternoon, "said George.

Cragen looked over at Officer Kay. She was sipping her coffee. She put down her cup and listened intently.

"You visited Miss Gallagher's parents in Beaverton? "

" Oh, yes," she said. "It was difficult telling her parents. The girl was old enough to be out on her own, but she must have led a sheltered life and still lived at home. They argued while I was there. One blamed the other for letting her go."

"Did she have any close friends or a love interest?" Cragen inquired.

"Oh, she was a loner---a couple of girls-- she went to high school with—but no boyfriend. I was able to get names and addresses and visited three of them. They had the same story—she was absolutely by herself most of the time. The girls accepted that this was the way Quinn was. They all loved her pretty voice and talent. And the only place she was at ease was on the stage. She turned into a different person completely then."

"And her tour on that ocean cruise ship?" Cragen interrupted.

"Yes, they did tell me about that. She very much enjoyed it. She certainly had a twinkle in her eye when she returned. They said she didn't say much about her experience there. Quinn was always that way—kept her thoughts to herself."

"George, when that captain gets back in on his next trip. Get him a message to call so we can talk to him about her previous cruise experiences."

"I will sir. He left us his cell number. I will call him." George then recalled their conversations with the band. "When we met with the band, we discovered that the leader and the other girl in the band were married. They had nothing bad to say about Quinn. They thought she was a great entertainer. We might keep the banjo player in mind as being rejected by Quinn. Could be a motive. She was a loner just like Kay said. We are getting the same reports everywhere. And, that captain, he seemed like he might have a roving eye—despite being married. I wouldn't doubt that. There didn't seem to be any other underlaying motives. Mary will let us know anything she finds out about the band members.

She will be playing with them for a while—at least till her new job comes in--police dispatch. Now, she's an undercover. I just discovered that Astoria Emergency Dispatch is short about six people. They came out with a notice that Dispatch will be combining with Seaside until they get the situation settled. They stated it is temporary, but who knows if they might not decide it is more cost efficient that way. We will see, Mary may not work in Astoria."

" I hadn't read that yet. It's hard to get help right now. Perhaps—when people run out of money—we will see a change," Cragen said." Nick, was there anything that the men found on the boat that would cause suspicion?"

"No, sir. We found nothing out of place. There were no scuffles, marks on the decks or railings Definitely, no blood! The dressing room was immaculate."

"Well, George, you do the supervising on the spaghetti search. Branch out and search all the town restaurants if you have to. Let see what we can find. If she was with anyone, get a composite drawing and description."

"Yes, sir! If anyone can draw faces, Jon can. We'll give it a good try."

Cragen ended the meeting asking for office help in tracing down Quinn's previous history. Officer Jan Spade, a new recruit, volunteered. She would trace out Miss Gallagher's previous history on the cruise ship if at all possible.

CHAPTER 11 SEARCHING ASTORIA:

When Nick arrived, the restaurant had just opened. It was afternoon. Fulio's was a popular place in the community. It had no large advertising sign to direct tourists to the door, although the locals all knew 'Fulios.'

(Fulio's Commercial Street)

The waiter met Officer Nick and Jon at the door. Diners were few because of the returned mask mandate. Officer Nick identified himself and his brother and they were taken to a small table in the back so they could talk. He took out a picture of Quinn for the waiter to look at. " Have you seen this girl? She would have been here on Thursday evening , the 16th of September."

"Yes, I did-- Too pretty to forget. She had that

green dress on too. She met a guy at the door. She greeted him with a hug—like she knew him well. They talked like they were well informed about each other—family, friends, etc. He had another girl with him in blue jeans and a sweatshirt. She had red hair also—might have been a sister. They were here about 45 minutes. He paid the bill and they left. He did pay with a visa."

Nick exclaimed on this new fact. "We can trace him. We can use that information."

"Did she use their names at any time?"

"I didn't hear any names. I get regulars. I have not seen any of them before. She said she had a little time before she had to be back at the boat. They were going to walk around Astoria a bit."

"Can you describe him?"

"He was about five' ten"- or eleven". He had dark hair and a little graying around the temples. He had a bit of an accent. I couldn't tell where from. We get so many people off boats and cruise ships. After a while, the accents begin to sound alike."

Jon took his art pad and they proceeded to get the details down on paper.

" Curly or straight hair, sir?" asked Jon.

" Very straight—with the grayish-white mixed in at the temples-very little."

"How dark was his skin?'

" He looked more like he had a deep tan—yes—I would describe him that way—not a ethnic thing--but more like a tan."

Jon showed the waiter his drawing. " What do you think about this?"

"That looks a lot like him—the nose is   different, and the hair line should be a little less receding."

It took Jon 20 minutes more to get it to the waiter's satisfaction.

"That's it. You got it. That's him!"

They both smiled.

Nick spoke up. "We will get a subpoena for the visa info and get back to you sir.   You've been a powerful help."

" I'm always here. We have short hours. Whoever did this does need to be stopped. I'm happy to help. Oh—and   something else. He was also quite well built—like an athlete or someone who had been out in the sun."

"How was he dressed?" Nick asked.

"Oh, nothing unusual—Kinda dark colored clothing. He wore a tee shirt, but it was black."

Both Nick and Jon walked out the door with a feeling that this could turn into some kind of a lead. They reported to George. And George took the information to CSI O'Neal.

CHAPTER 12 SUPECT WITHOUT A NAME:

It was Wednesday. After their discussion of the visit to Fulio's, Cragen said, "I want you to get a subpoena for Fulio's so we can obtain a credit card receipt and also for the card company. This is a solid lead and a good description. First let's look at the video feeds the captain gave us. I'll pull it up and put in the password. They were definitely saved. Let's see if we can spot this fellow."

" We've got a video also that Mary took-- but it is just one of their performances. I haven't looked at it yet," said George.

"Yes. Might be something usable. This composite sketch that the waiter gave us-he said that he was definitely there with Miss Gallagher. We will have a go at identifying this guy ourselves first. If we let this slip out, we could be in for false leads that would impede this investigation."

" You're right sir. I agree. It could delay it. Humm. He looks like the captain."

"Could be but I don't think that his hairline matches. Course, witnesses can be wrong too. I'm going to send Kay to Beaverton tomorrow to show this to Quinn's parents."

"Good idea. They may have seen him!"

"Get the   subpoena first thing in the morning,

George."

"I will sir." Weariness was catching up with him. He and Mary had spent too much time talking into the early hours of this day He was tired! She got to sleep in!

CHAPTER 13 THE CAMERAS:

It took them all the next day to go over every camera on both decks for the day of the murder.

They paid close attention to the band and paused at each black-haired man and noted the location place on video.

'My Bonnie' was outfitted for trips without lodging. Staterooms existed for the crew and a nice dressing room with a cot and chairs for the band- a small kitchen area and ½ bath.

Up to 8:00 Am: loading for the first trip.

All was as expected.

When the band came on board, they were all friendly to each other. No problems there. Captain-- tanned and athletic with hair graying around the temples.

Rory McDowell—also darker skin but no graying. He had dark hair and eyes. The video showed his wife, Maddie, talking to Quinn Gallagher. They looked quite friendly.

Adam and Danny looked much too young—but yes, they had dark hair also.

The band members were dressed in green. Adam and Danny carried their instruments in. The others had left them on the stage. They all looked in good spirits. No problems here!

10:00 AM: Two hours on shore in Astoria.

12:00 noon: loading back on board

1:30: Portland/ end of trip

Up to 3:00 PM. second trip loading with new passengers.

They noted something different on the 3:00 PM departure. They had seen Maddie argue with her husband but could not determine what she was saying. He just shrugged his shoulders and turned and walked away. She was not happy. And when she went to the stage, she ignored everyone and seemed to be sulking through their performance. No one noticed her as the bass player was always at the back of the stage. She had recovered fully by the end of the show. Quinn had five duet numbers with Rory McDowell. They wondered if Rory's wife was showing a bit of a jealous streak.

At times, guests would stop and talk with the band. They noted that towards the end of their set, a dark-haired man came up to Quinn with a newspaper in his hand and flipped over to a page which he showed her. She looked startled. He spoke to her dramatically and left. They could not determine if he was the suspect due to the grainy video. "Can we zoom in and enlarge that one?" George asked.

O'Neal tried his best with no success. " If this comes up as important, we will get one of the experts."

5:00 PM: Docking at Astoria --Rory and his wife left together. She moved fast and was ahead of him a half-dozen steps—again upset again it seemed. The other two band members left together. Quinn Gallagher left by herself as did the captain.

5:00 Pm: The trip boarded quickly before that time. The band had found each other on return and was in good spirits. Quinn was not with them!

At the last minute, Quinn Gallagher appeared out of breath and running up the plankway. No one followed. She did not go straight to the bandstand. She headed to the right instead and was out of view.

There was a camera which showed the band quarters. They were moving in and out. Maddie got there late. She had a plate of food. The others also headed for the buffet one or two at a time. They were not scheduled to play right way.

Questions for the band: Did Quinn find them on her arrival?

Questions for the captain: Was anyone missing of the returning guests?

And to all of the Astoria Police Department: Who is the suspect?

CHAPTER 14 SEARCHING FOR THE SUSPECT:

Officer Kay had spent the day in Beaverton visiting the parents of Miss Gallagher. They had settled in with their loss and tried to help Kay as much as they could. She showed them the sketch of the suspect. Then she moved on to as many of Quinn's friends as she could find available-- to see if they could help her at all.

"Sir, it was a wasted trip. None of the Beaverton people could ID our suspect. There was one woman who hemmed and hawed a bit when she saw the sketch, but she was not sure she could make an ID. We could return to her if we have further details come up."

CSI O'Neal replied, "This has been a frustrating business tracking this guy down. We got the info from Fulio's and also went to the credit card company." Our suspect has used his visa card various places—6 months in England, also in Astoria and Portland. It's gonna be hard to trace. He has his address in Astoria—but it's a PO box. We have someone posted down at the Post Office to see if we can catch him there. Previous address was in Forest Grove, Oregon. We checked there also. It was a young man in one of those million-dollar houses—no furniture, just computers and a half-dozen chairs. He did not resemble our man at all.

His name was the same as the one on the card —a Jacob Ellsworth. I am suspecting he had some kind of internet scheme going. If that were my district, I'd be checking it out closely. I did give the Police department there a call to let them know my suspicions." He continued as he stood. "I've got the receipts together. I will let you take care of this, Kay--telephone work of course. England would be a suitable location to pin down these charges. You can call the businesses. Quinn was in that area as a musician on an ocean cruise. If we can place them together somewhere, we'll be ahead for sure. Did her parents say anything about the overseas cruise?"

"Yes, they did. Let me look at my notes." Kay pulled a notepad out of her purse, flipped it and said, "It was before the Covid scenario-- looks like the winter of 2019 right up to when they shut down the cruises. Because of that, I am guessing that she was off work for a time till the captain started his river cruise. He called her."

"Yes, she was off work—stopped the cruise in March of 2020. So, she had about three months of no work." Cragen mentioned. He walked across the room. "I'm going to get Jacob posted on our suspect wallboard now that I've got a name. It's getting a bit heavy —the band, the captain. We keep finding suspects, don't we?"

"Yes, well sir, I'm going to get right on this. I still have the afternoon. I can get more details for us.

"Thanks, Kay."

CHAPTER 15 MORE INFORMATION:

Meantime, your author and guest were fortunate enough to hear from a source about what was said on the boat about Quinn Gallagher's past history. Here it is—as I know it.

George had been asked to set up an appointment with the captain and the band when they arrived back in Astoria. CSI O'Neal and himself would be there when the boat got in at three. George grabbed his briefcase and he and Cragen drove to the pier and parked. Passengers were oft-loading. The boat would be quiet until they returned.

Captain Murphy met them on the deck. "Have you discovered anything yet about Quinn?"

"It is starting to come together." Cragen said. We are finding that her history needs exploring for sure! What can you tell us about the cruise ship you both were on?"

Captain Murphy directed them aboard the boat. "Let's go below deck so we can talk." He opened a door and they followed him downstairs to a large section. They found a table facing out to the river. Cragen noted this area had no camera.

"We were based out of Copenhagen, Denmark. It was a nine-day cruise—went to Berlin, Germany-St. Peterburg, Russia, Finland. It was nice. Quinn fitted right in with a jazz band. She can-could do any kind of music. The ship was huge. It could carry thousands of passengers. I was working with the crew. In fact, I had worked myself up the ladder pretty good—then Covid shut us down. We all went home."

"Was she involved with anyone?" Cragen looked out the windows at the river.

"We have free time on a cruise. The band is usually scheduled when the passengers come back on board. So, they did go off the ship sometimes for the day. I did too. It can get boring however—same stops over and over during the season. We just hung around the ship most days, however. Quinn met a young man and they developed quite a relationship. They liked each other. He took the cruise a number of times—don't know if that was because he met Quinn. Might have been."

"Did you get his name?"

"It was Jake-something. I noted they visited St. Peterburg every time he came on the cruise. He didn't have interest in the other stops."

"Hmmm, that's interesting. Can you describe him?"

" Well, he was dark haired, average height—decent shape physically."

George pulled out the sketch book." Does this look like him?"

"Yes, that is a good likeness. I saw him here once

talking to Quinn at the bandstand the night she disappeared. So, they were still in contact. He must be an American."

When they left the boat, Cragen nodded to George. "This is getting strange! Why did Jacob turn up on this boat?"

"Sir, when we find him, we might be able to put this case together."

"You can bet we will." They left and went toward the band's dressing room. They asked everyone to leave and interviewed Rory, the band leader first.

CSI O'Neal asked the question they both had. "What was the argument that you and your wife had that last evening?"

"I bet the camera caught it—yes?"

"It did. Was it serious?"

Rory nodded his head in agreement. "She has been getting overly concerned and jealous lately. I have no interest in anyone but her. She confronted me because Quinn and I did so many Irish numbers together. Quinn was so good—of course we enjoyed singing together. It made the show. Her sense of harmony was so precise. There was a blend of our voices.   I could only attribute that to Quinn. I'm not that good!"

George looked over at him. "Had your wife ever done this before?"

"Never, it surprised me! Quinn and I did stand really close to harmonize and we always played to the audience. I'm afraid Maddie got fixated on that nearness we had. I was a little neglectful in that I had promised her that she could do a duet with me or a solo for herself. I haven't dealt with that as I should have." He seemed quite sincere. "Now that we have Mary Bell, I'm afraid the same situation is happening. I am concerned."

At that point, Cragen told Rory he could go and asked his wife to step in. She did and sat down in the nearest chair.

George confronted her right away. "Mrs. McDowell, we are concerned about the video we watched where you are having a disagreement with your husband. What happened there?"

Maddie tried to make light of the situation but did not succeed. "Oh, I know it's silly. I don't know why I have these feelings." Her mood changed. Maddie was in tears. "Rory's never given me any reason to mistrust him, but he was just so close to Quinn." Her hand shook as she emphasized that point. "I could see that leading to a further affection to her, I just warned him. That's all."

"Did you threaten him?"

"No, of course not. I love him so much! I just didn't want anything to happen to our marriage."

Cragen cut in. " You seemed to be upset all the way

through your performance that night."

"Yes, I'm afraid I was. I couldn't help it! I try to put our music first. I just could not do it that afternoon. I kept thinking—what if?"

"What if?"

"If he and Quinn had gotten further involved? I didn't want anything to happen to our marriage. I'm three months pregnant. I'm going to have to be off for a while, I know! This baby will mean so much to us! What happens when I need to be off?"

They concluded the discussion asking about what happened when they left the boat.

"Well, usually we are together. Quinn said she was meeting someone. Rory and I went off together. We ate lunch at the Labor Temple. They have such good hamburgers. We ate lite later at the buffet."

"And the guys?" Cragen tossed that red lock of hair out of his face.

"Don't know where they went." Rory and I stayed together the whole time-- till it was time to board."

"Thank you, Mrs. McDowell. We may talk to you later if we have more questions."

They left the room. My guest and I—when we heard about it—both felt that she sounded quite uneasy to be questioned that way. Was she a suspect?

CHAPTER 16 LIFE GOES ON IN ASTORIA:

The month of September finished with no more details for the police to research. Officer Kay had thoroughly checked out her information and given CSI O'Neal all she could about Jacob's visa charges that he made. Officer Jan had nothing unusual to report about Quinn's time in Europe.

The officers were still searching Astoria and watching the post office box to find the elusive fellow who was at Fulio's that night. Then the big Columbia Crossing happened on October tenth. The Astoria Bridge is shut down to traffic. They run over four miles (or walk) from Washington to Oregon every year. This year officers made it a point to search through all two thousand runners. It was a smaller crowd than the previous years because of Covid. But, because the man was in such good physical shape, he might have been there. They normally used their motorcycles to cover this event anyhow, so it was not noticeable by the runners that they all had a sketch of the man and an extra mission for that day. Nothing turned up.

Mary Bell stayed with the band. The boat was going to keep coming to Astoria as long as it could—through rainy weather and all. She left a complete report of her time with the Irish band often. It was a much-needed report and Officer Kay processed and explored each one. October was especially rainy —but this year it was wetter than most Octobers. There was a windstorm or two but mostly just rain. You would see an occasional tourist with an umbrella. Locals didn't use them.

Emerald Heights, a local apartment complex on the east end of Astoria—just out of town-- put on a 'Boo Bash.' Christina Beldon, Community Manager, stated that they were honoring Officer Sam Whisler who died of natural causes in July at the age of twenty-six. She stated that he was quite active in planning the event and that he cared about the community. The 'Bash' included games for kids, and a focus on a costume contest. It was also a fund raiser for his family.

We also extend our sympathy to his family and friends and to the Astoria Police force.

The Lighthouse Christian Church on the highway to Seaside had a special 'Trunk or Treat' event for the kids also.

The community was awash with spooky events. Jeff Daly's 'Astoria underground' and Gulley's Butcher Shop 'Ghost Tours' were events that were scheduled and sold out.

Downtown stores were giving out candy as they did every year. This year it was on Saturday, although Halloween was on a Sunday. It was sponsored by the Astoria Downtown Historic District Association.

Despite the Covid-19 crisis, Astoria enjoyed holidays and family traditions.

And in the middle of all this activity, Officer George Van , after taking his specialized training class, was given his detective position in the Astoria Police Department. Mary Bell attended the special ceremony with officers on the force on November 1st. She dressed in her favorite blue and white dress and had given extra attention to curling her long blond hair. She chose their seating well. As she was so very small, they sat in the front so she could see. George was given the keys to his new office and also the title of Sergeant Van, Detective. He would be managing cases throughout the county and base his work at the Astoria Police Department. Mary tossed her blond hair back and smiled as George accepted the honor.

Likewise, with the retirement of Dr Summer as medical examiner, CSI O'Neal took over that position to go with his job of Crime Scene Investigator. Cragen and George continued to work together well.

CHAPTER 17 WE SEE A BREAK!

In celebration, Mary and George had planned a big dinner at the Silver Salmon Grill.

CSI O'Neal was to have dinner with his family and close friends that evening. This afternoon, however, he called retired Dr Summers to meet him in the morgue so that the doctor could brief him on Quinn Gallagher's death. He pointed out pictures of the body, the injury report, and showed him all the paperwork.

" I don't see a report on the fingerprints. Is it here somewhere?"

" No, these are the prints, but it wasn't necessary to send them out. The parents identified her right away. They were broken-hearted. That's the worst part of this job—seeing the damage it does to those around the victim. I almost cried myself. They certainly did!"

"Did they stay very long with her?"

"They said they couldn't. They couldn't bear it. They left right away."

Cragen asked Dr Summers to send out the fingerprints for paperwork. He would take care of putting them in the files although he didn't think it was that necessary at this late date. Dr Summers said he would do that immediately.

Yes, the next day it finally happened! This was kept very secretive, so we did not find out about this until later. Officer Nick found the elusive Jacob Ellsworth at the local Safeway Store—buying personal items. He wore a hoodie and the needed covid-19 mask for shopping. Since Nick had been with the waiter at Fulio's when he described him, he had no problem at all identifying him—even with the disguise. He took him into custody immediately and they went directly to the station.

Both Cragen and George were together discussing the case when he entered the office.

"Here he is! Found him at Safeway." He proudly beamed.

"Well, excellent job, Nick. Are you sure it's him?"

"Definitely---credit card and ID in billfold."

"Take him to the interrogation room. We will both be right down."

Jacob Ellsworth sat back in his chair planning what to say to the officers. He had to decide, and it looks like he would have to take them into his confidence. This had been an ordeal for him. When he talked to Quinn at the bandstand, he had arranged to meet her at Fulio's. She had avoided letting anyone know where she was going or who she was meeting.

The two officers walked into the room, and he got up out of his chair to acknowledge their entrance.

Cragen was first to speak. " You are Jacob Ellsworth? We need to know about you and Quinn Gallagher."

"Yes, I can explain. I can!"

"What do you need to explain, Mr. Ellsworth?"

"I need your help."

"You might need more than our help. Do you want us to call a lawyer?"

"No! Definitely not!" He nodded his head as he spoke. " Let's not bring any more people into this situation. It is dangerous at this point."

"Dangerous?"

"Quinn and I are CIA agents. We've been working on a case overseas from a cruise ship—it involves a spy ring—double agent spies."

George and Cragen both opened their mouths in surprise. "What?" they said in unison.

"Yes, that's right--a spy ring. Quinn and I are CIA agents." He emphasized this again. "We've been working on this case in St. Petersburg, Russia—until Covid shut us down. We had about closed it."

" Can you prove you are CIA? I can hardly believe that!"

"No problem, let me write down a number. You can check that. In fact, before we go any further, you should do that. This is my boss. His name is Ivan Johansen. You have my phone. You will find an encrypted number that goes directly to the CIA offices. They are based in Langley, Virginia at the George Bush Center for Intelligence. Do the verification. I've nowhere to go. I could use a cup of coffee, however."

" I'll have one sent in, "George answered.

George and Cragen both went out shaking their heads in disbelief—the CIA in Astoria, Oregon. No! George stopped at the desk and ordered coffee sent in and they proceeded to O'Neal's office.

" What is he telling us? Do you believe that?"George said as they approached Cragen's desk

No, I can't—not probable. Let's check him out anyhow. This will take a while."

"Maybe he's just stalling."

"Could be."

We learned later that the two officers did verify that phone number. The CIA also did investigating to be sure that they were talking to the Astoria police. Then they gave them the go-ahead for Ivan Johansen to talk with them. Our Astoria Police Office received a copy of Jake's fingerprints so they could verify the man they were holding as Jake Ellsworth. They talked with Jake's boss. He stated that Jake would fill them in, but anything they learned should be considered classified. No one should know unless there was a need to know. He would need their help indeed.

Before going into the interrogation room, Cragen stopped and informed Officer Nick that he was to keep Jake's arrest secret. No one was to know that he was in custody. If he had told anyone, he was to make sure they were told the man was released and was not a suspect. Nick told them he had not told anyone about the arrest as of yet.

Jake was napping with his head on the table when they came in. He quickly went on alert as if there was something about which he should be concerned. It was his habit. In his business, there was always a need to be aware of surroundings. He recovered quickly and greeted the two.

"Well?" He said.

Cragen answered. "You are certainly a CIA agent. How about telling us the whole story?"

" First, I have to inform you that what you are hearing is very confidential. It starts like this. Quinn and I were on an undercover operation on a cruise ship in Europe. You know about that cruise already —but you don't know what it was all about. We were after a spy ring—and there were double agents involved. These people were in close contact with the Russians in St. Petersburg. This was our mission —to find out the information so this country could locate and arrest the spy team. There were about a dozen spies. I think the contact with St Petersburg was so that they could have training. They had about 8 hours to do that when the ship docked.

We were both on their tail each time they went off the ship. And we both watched them on board also. We got names. We got addresses. We turned them into our office and the majority were arrested. Some are still under surveillance at this time. This also involved drugs. We think that the drug money was used to finance their operations. We also caught five of the crew in the act of loading the drugs onto the ship. We got those names. These guys were arrested also. We still have our eye on Captain Murphy. He could be involved. Quinn had talked Captain Murphy into recommending her to the Irish band on the river cruise boat. He did not suspect anything."

"Wow," said George. " I would not have ever suspected that our small town would be involved in something this big!"

"But it is certainly sad that you lost Miss Gallagher. She was certainly a talent, we hear."

"No, we didn't actually." Jake leaned in towards the two officers. "Since we actually have no authority to arrest, we had to involve the FBI to help us out. Quinn is alive! The girl that was involved was an exact FBI double—after she died her hair red. I hated to see that happen. FBI agents are equipped for that sort of surveillance. She was armed. She was always on guard. I don't see how she could have let an agent get to her. It seems improbable. Two of the spy ring guys are in the wind. They know about me and Quinn. They know our names. They know I am hiding in Astoria, and they are actively searching for me. They don't know Quinn is alive."

Both George and Cragen were startled at the news. They were sitting at the table with mouths open in surprise. It took them a moment to react.

"Dr Summers did not run this lady's fingerprints. We had a positive ID from her parents. So, he didn't bother. I'm running them now. This killer— how could he make such a mistake?" Cragen showed bewilderment.

"Your department made the same mistake. I met her; she was identical. I could have also been confused at first glance. After we ate dinner at Fulio's, Quinn changed her dress and her double put that green dress on. She had to run to make the boat. Red-headed- green dress-played the guitar and could sing. She was perfect! I'm sorry we lost her. How could they have gotten to us so fast?"

"So, where are you now?"

"We're at a house over on Franklin by Safeway. We have FBI agents guarding us in every room and outside. We want to spring a trap to catch these guys. So, we will need your help."

"How can we help? Do you have photos of the two double agents?" said George.

No. But first inform Quinn's parents that she is alive. Let them know that you will fill them in on details as soon as you can. Quinn can call them also. Then leak the story to the newspaper and radio stations by having someone tell them that the lady was mistakenly identified, and that the department is actively looking for Quinn and her boyfriend who are still in town-- should be enough to get the spies back here."

"We will certainly do that. Her parents are going to be happy!" George said.

"How—how did you find out about them being after you?" Cragen added.

"It was a newspaper in London. The news article was about the capture of the spy ring. And someone leaked our names out. I showed it to Quinn on the boat. We knew we had to do something. So, Quinn and I arranged to meet on her break at the restaurant. I filled her in on what I was doing. I had already got hold of the FBI. They knew also and they were sending agents to Astoria. Quinn's double was already there waiting for us at the restaurant in mid-town Astoria. We have to testify—or the case could collapse. Quinn and I are actually engaged. That happened on the cruise ship. I've got double concern for her safety, of course. Right now, we are under witness protection, and I hope that is not going to be a permanent thing. Our careers are at risk."

Cragen tossed his red hair out of his eyes for the third time and said, "I can see where you are in serious danger right now."

"Yes, we are!"

I was called to the station. Your author is now sitting here taking all this new information in like a fly on the wall. I had my guest with me. The police department has enlisted our help to 'leak' the story to the media without revealing too much. Now we've got the details of a real mystery. CSI Cragen is now reporting everything about the case with our promise to not publish until they were finished. And —we are keeping it confidential. They know we can be a help to them. We leaked the fact that the dead lady was not Quinn. We also leaked the fact that the police were looking for the two of them. We may do more!

CSI Cragen: "Before we use you on this case, DeLores May, we need to know something about the lady you have with you."

DeLores May: "Of course, that is important. This is Abigail Ruby. She has been my friend for about five years now. I met her when she first rented an apartment from us. That was in 2018. She is close to my age. She's 85.The last couple of years she has lived in Scappoose, Oregon. It's about seventy-four miles away on Highway 30. She recently purchased a new vehicle--a SUV. She is ready to roll to the coast more often now."

George: "Neither of you ladies look eighty-five. I would estimate maybe—60's."

DeLores May: " Why thank you, George. You have become my most favorite person in Astoria. We are in decent shape—just moving slower than we used to."

Cragen: "Sometime I don't do so well getting around either. I can feel it in my bones! Tell me something about yourself, Ms. Ruby."

Abigail: "Well, I worked a full 40 years for 'Ax Filings.' It's a computer company that manages company file work. I loved my job. I quit when I was seventy-five. I did author a book or two. Now, I'm just enjoying my retirement. DeLores has so many interesting places to show me. I so enjoy being here-- and these mysteries that are happening? I feel like I'm part of the team. I do appreciate that!"

Cragen: "Do you have a family? "

Abigail: "No, sorry to say. I never had the privilege. It was always work for me. I envy DeLores at times." She tossed her hair back. It was very gray and did in a bun in the back, but it did have an annoying wisp which seemed to pop up when she least expected it. "I will enjoy this. We can be of help, do you think?"

George: "I'm sure you will be."

George turned toward Cragen. "Sir, we have DeLores May's prints, but I think Abigail's prints should also be on file. This last go-a-round we found more unknown prints. The staff is checking them out now. If we had hers, we could eliminate them for sure. It would help!"

Cragen: " Yes, that is a fine idea. Ok, Ms. Ruby?"

Abigail: "Well, I guess so—willing to help."

Cragen: "Welcome to this team, Abigail! Just remember everything is hush-hush."

DeLores May: "You can be sure that she will be very quiet about this. It is important."

Abigail: "I'm like a fly on the wall."

AND WE ARE LEFT WITH QUESTIONS
1. Who killed the red-headed FBI agent?
2. Are Quinn and Jake in real danger or is the FBI enough to protect them.
3. Is Captain Murphy really a drug dealer?

ABIGAIL RUBY   A HELP FOR THE CASE
(PHOTO BY CLEMENT ALIZE- UNSPLASH)

CHAPTER 18 STORMY NOVEMBER:

The weather had been quite warm and rainy-averaging in the 50's. Mid November brought flooding in all lowland areas. We were informed by 'The Astorian' newspaper that the Coast Guard was responsible for rescuing campers at an RV park on the coast at Sakowin. RVs were sitting in water about six inches deep and in parts of the park the water had risen to four feet. In near-by Otis, another RV park was also flooded. The Coast Guard stated that they had rescued a dozen people and three dogs that Friday. Local responders evacuated at least eight. Campers were being woke up to the warning from car horns early in the morning. Those Coast Guard helicopters were also responsible for saving a woman by rescuing her out of a swollen river. Thank you, Coast Guard!

OUR BACKYARD (Courtesy of Diana and Glenn Gulley)

A record two inches of rain had fallen that Thursday —the most rain for that date in 70 years-- and the rain continued non-stop. November has broken all records!

Astoria suffered a waterline break, They considered that it may have been caused by movement in the earth because of all the heavy rains. There was localized flooding. Culverts and pipes got backed up, especially out on the road to Olney. Roads flooded in low-lying areas. Also, about a thousand customers lost power because of the storm on Thursday afternoon.

And the rains continued! We didn't know it then, but January would have even worse flooding.

The river in this kind of weather is most beautiful and it certainly fun to be on a boat. We decided to take the early afternoon cruise from Astoria to Portland on the 'My Bonnie.' We could be of help with the case. We now know all the details. We will see what we can find out! You might say we, also, were acting as spies!

The captain greeted us. We followed him across the plank. He was carrying a bag about the size of a backpack. We wondered about that and were whispering to ourselves why he needed it. We caught up to him. "Captain?"

"Yes, ma'am. I am the captain." He stepped aside. "What can I do for you?"

I spoke up. "I'm DeLores May, and this is—(mumble, mumble). Is it possible to take this cruise in the other direction? We live here. We've been hearing good things about this trip!"

"Yes, we have room going back and by the looks of reservations, we will not be full on our return trip either. Let's step inside this door. Someone from my crew will sign you up."

"Oh, that's so nice. We were so hoping we could do this. The weather—the rain—so nice on the river." I slipped slightly on the ramp but grabbed the rail in time. I had to be careful because of my sensitive left leg. I had taken more than one fall in the last couple of years.

"It has been said that winter is the best time to be on a boat. The river is beautiful this time of year. There is seating inside by the windows to keep you dry— and the band will be playing shortly. This is John, our ticket master."

John got his passenger list out so he could sign us up. "Thank you, Captain," my guest said.

I thanked him also and he left to go to his quarters. It was a most enjoyable trip setting. We prepared a plate of luscious food at the buffet and went to a table on the north side. It looked like we could see more of the shoreline and a few cities—and a glimpse of the band through those front windows. The band was protected from the weather also. We could see Mary Bell tuning up her tenor guitar. The other members were doing likewise. She was smiling back at Maddie and having a conversation. She seemed happy and in her element. Rory, Maddie's husband, was now joining in. The band seemed quite compatible and friendly to each other.

"Yes, this table is perfect! We can see about everything." I said.

We looked across the water. There was the Arrow 2 tugboat out on a maritime history tour. Plans are to make it an attraction year around. Captain Mark Schachter restored the boat and started tours in the spring. It's located in Warrenton just across the bridge. It's complete with a heated cabin and restrooms. "I read something about that. I'd like to go one day."

Abigail agreed. "The three-hour tour is well worth it. Look, here's his number on the board! (503) 791-6250. And his e mail arrowtug@gmail.com. Let's look into that."

(Photo by Captain Mark Schachter)

(Tug at Skipanon marina in Warrenton)
The trip to Portland was uneventful but nice. We enjoyed the strains of 'Danny Boy and Molly Malone.' Every once in a while, I can feel my Irish heritage kick in. Such enjoyment of the music is usually when it happens. The music coming from that beautiful fiddle is so typical of Ireland and I so envy his skill. My old antique fiddle sets at home gathering dust while I'm off on a career of writing.

"Oh, her singing is beautiful!" my guest commented.

"Yes, it is! Mary Bell is Sergeant George's fiancé. You met him this morning."

"Yes, I did. He's so tall and she's so short! How did that romance ever happen?"

"Mutual admiration, I guess. She was one of the suspects in that high-profile murder case a couple of months ago. They seemed to click right away."

" I love that! What a wonderful thing to happen."

" Yes, it is."

The boat was docking, and passengers were making ready to debark. I noticed that Captain Murphy had gotten his bag and he was in the crowd leaving the boat. It was the same bag.

" Let's follow him—see where he goes," I whispered to Abigail.

" You know, I will always follow you. You are taking me on a grand adventure. I love it!"

We headed down the ramp keeping the captain in our sight. He moved slow enough as if he had all day-very nonchalantly. It was a good thing because our legs were much shorter—and we were so much older.

He turned a corner. We carefully followed. He hadn't seen us.

There was a brick house in the middle of the next block. He rang a doorbell and stepped in. We walked past the house and behind a bush that was on the street. We could see easily from here. And we waited —15 minutes. _____

Captain Murphy came out of the house and headed back towards the boat. He had no bag! We still waited. As he rounded the corner, we stepped out, passed the house and wrote down the number. This information might be needed.

The rain had stopped! A little coffee shop was just ahead. So, this was a place to rest our feet. We picked a corner booth—where no one was near--ordered coffee and a sweet roll. "I think I will call CSI O'Neal in Astoria and let him know about this. What do you think?"

Abigail nodded. "I think we should. This is very suspicious."

"Remember what he said? The captain was suspected of drug dealing."

"Yes, I remember! I would love to write this book myself. Would you consider co-authoring it?"

I didn't want to crush her enthusiasm, so I told her maybe. She was such a nice lady and she had authored books before. "I'd like to read your books before I make up my mind. Will you get the information for me on where to get them?"

Abigail shrugged. " I course-- I will! I wrote them under a pseudonym. I can get you copies—may take me a couple of weeks."

"That's ok. I'll enjoy reading them."

"They are romance novels—not mysteries. I love writing. I'll order them today."

CSI O'Neal was glad to get our call. It was most certainly important. He took the address and the description of the bag and would call the Portland police. With our report, there was enough to get a warrant and search the property. He called them and waited!

It isn't always easy to solve a case like this.

We see it come together in, oh, so many ways,

The captain is a druggie, the ladies are on clue.

They are working on the case, but little they can do.

They can't carry big guns. They are
helpless against big guys.

They can only report their finding

And help solve the case in disguise.

CHAPTER 19 COOPERATION OR NOT?:

There had been situations where the Astoria Police Department had the help of the Portland police. Crimes often involve more than one city. If it was drugs, where did they come from? We know that the USCG ship 'Steadfast' had been responsible for stopping drugs from getting into the United States. Their ship was responsible for the collection of millions of dollars' worth of Cocaine alone. But it was such a huge business that they couldn't stop them all and drugs did get through in cities up and down the West Coast.

When Cragen called the Portland police, they did not waste time. They went directly to the docks, found the house, arrested three suspects after searching the house. They found the cocaine! It was still in the bag that we could identify. There was too much to even consider this was for their use. They were middlemen and had their own business selling. It didn't even take much time for them to give up the captain in order to get reduced sentences.

In turn, when 'My Bonnie' returned to Astoria, George and Cragen were there to arrest the captain and hold the ship at port. No one left the boat. The police department had gotten a warrant for searching the boat again. This time they concentrated on the crew, but they did not neglect searching each guest. Were any of them involved or was Captain Murphy in this all alone?

He refused to give anyone up. He refused to turn in the money, and he refused to cooperate with the police in any way. He sat in the interrogation room after asking for his lawyer to come from Portland. That was his stance. He also said he was not the killer. He had high respect for Quinn. He did not know that it was not Quinn Gallagher after all!

CHAPTER 20 MY BONNIE IS DOCKED:

We can see 'My Bonnie' sitting in the Columbia River from where we are parked. She is anchored and still. She will not move until she is searched again by the force. And we were also searched to avoid suspicion that we had anything to do with the arrest of the captain. Then we were let go.

Guests are upset. They had planned to see Astoria during these two hours. Instead, they see the yellow buses lined up to drive them back to Portland as soon as they are released. Mothers are scurrying after kids who had found the extra time on the boat as a fun-time to run and play with others their size. The officers evaluated every guest, took names and address and ID's. Each one was checked out at the police department with national files. Each one was also searched. Nothing was left undone. Names were to be matched at the station with the list of the names who were on the ship the day of the murder. Soon the buses pulled away and only the crew and the band were left. The passengers all were not considered to be involved to any extent at this time.

Both groups were quite cooperative. They agreed to help the Astoria Police Department any way they could.

The crew numbered twenty. The band stayed except for Mary Bell. It would be a while before they would be released.

George had enlisted the help of the 'sniffer dogs' that are owned by Diana and Glenn Gulley. Ruby found some cocaine hidden in a cabinet and Rosie found the money stored in the floorboards in the captain's quarters.

Ruby and Rosie on the way to work

CHAPTER 21 THE CREW AND THE BAND:

Information was found. It took a few short hours to completely search the boat and get any needed information from the twenty-four left there.

They were searching not only for information about the drugs, but they were also looking for a murderer —or information of any kind about the murder.

Nick and Jon were questioning each one of the crew while Cragen and George brought each band member into their dressing room—separately again.

They would do this and then talk to them all together to see if anything else popped up.

Cragen: "Mr. McDowell, You said you left the boat the night of the murder at 5:00 PM with your wife? How about the others?"

Rory: "Well. We left together. Our two other guys left together also—Danny and Adam."

Cragen: " Were you with your wife the entire time until performance time?"

Rory: "Yes, I was with—oh, no. She did go to the restroom right before show-time."

Cragen: "Did she seem rushed when she came back-upset or anything?"

Rory: "No-course not. She got back in plenty of time."

Cragen: "Everyone else back on time?"

Rory: "Yes, they all had time to spare."

George: "So Mrs. McDowell, on the night of the murder, were you and your husband together the whole time."

Maddie: " Of course we were. We told you that last time we spoke."

George: " And he never left your sight?"

Maddie: "No, he didn't. We were together."

Maddie seemed quite ill at ease throughout her interrogation.

They had both been questioned on their whereabouts. George and Cragen were concerned that there was a difference in the two stories.

Danny Malone, Banjo player and Adam Reilly, Mandolist individually had a contradiction as well. Danny said that the two had parted company downtown for about an hour. Adam said they were together.

The officers both ushered everyone into the room. They then told the band about the conflicting statements they had made.

Maddie: "Yes of course, I forgot. I did go to the

restroom. I was only gone five minutes."

George: " We noted that you have a bathroom in your dressing room. Why didn't you use that?"

Maddie: "Oh, I just don't know. We went by the restroom, and I just went in. I was-like I said—only gone for five. Sorry for my forgetfulness!"

George: " So actually. You cannot vouch for your husband during that time?"

Maddie: "Fraid I can't."

Cragen: "And you two fellers, why do we have a disagreement here?"

Adam: "I did step into a bar for a few minutes. I don't think it was an hour, though."

Cragen: "So you two cannot vouch for each other either?"

Danny: " Like I said—it was an hour. I just walked around the streets—street things going on. We met back at the boat."

Cragen: " Now all of you. Was there any other time when you could not place one of the band members?"

Adam: "I did miss Maddie right after we came in."

Danny: "Same here. It must have been longer than five minutes. Oh, and we did go out for the buffet---all of us at various times."

Cragen and George walked out shaking their heads

about the confused statements. They released the crew to take the boat back to Portland with a warning to stay in that city. They might need to talk to them again. They asked Maddie McDowell to come to the station for further statements. They would get her back to Portland as soon as possible.

"I'll come too, Maddie." Rory McDowell said. "And I'll get us an attorney."

George said, "don't you worry. We will treat her well. She is not a suspect at this time."

" I want to be with her. I will get that attorney."

Back at the station, Cragen called the   investigative team together for a meeting to discuss their findings.

"Looks like the four band members are already on our board as suspects. Maddie McDowell is the top suspect right now. She is in the interrogation room with her attorney, and I will be interviewing her after this briefing is over. They did not agree on the time elements. Lucy, would you make sure their pictures are on that board? Also include Captain Murphey."

 Also, he said, "as a 'need to know', I would like to inform this task force of a number of pertinent facts. You are not to let this get out at any time--- very important. You noted that the paper had a little information on the murdered girl not being Quinn. We leaked that purposely. This office is working with the FBI and the CIA."

A murmur went up amid the group.

He continued. " Yes, that is a fact. No one knows that and we have to do our best to support them. It involves a spy ring that Quinn and Jake were tracking down out of Russia. They managed to get enough on them where the FBI did arrest them all except two and they have been under a threat since. Those two are looking actively for our heroes. Jake and Quinn have guards to protect them, and they hope to catch these guys. They are the only

witnesses. The case would fall apart if something happened to them. Then there is the drug case against the Captain. They could not get enough evidence against him overseas—yes, they were on a cruise ship and watching him closely too. We got him --thanks to our writer and her friend."

He nodded his head as everyone headed out the door. "Kay, how did Quinn's parents take the news?"

Well. "Sir, you should have been there. They were so happy. I was glad to bring them that news—very much so!"

"Here's something that may be new to all of you." Cragen spoke with authority.   "Keep it also as classified. Police Chief Geoff Spalding is thinking of retiring. He has been at police work for a good long time. I'm sure you have heard the rumors. It will be a lengthy process. He will stay with us till the new guy comes on board."

We were sitting in on the briefing and later discovered that he made official notice on December 15th when it came out in the Astoria newspaper.

CHAPTER 22 A VIABLE SUSPECT:

Maddie's interrogation was started after her and her husband had consulted with an Astoria attorney. He convinced Maddie that she should tell the officers exactly what happened. If she volunteered now, it would go much easier with her. The Police Department was only interested in what actually happened. So—she should report that. Rory agreed. They were going to have to make the best of this and telling the truth was the only way to go!

Rory introduced their attorney, Jason Onyx.

Maddie began. "I should have told you this right from the start! Those few minutes I was gone need to be dealt with. I was coming out of the restroom. She had just walked up the plank and had turned the corner. I don't know why I did it, but I confronted her about Rory again and I pushed her—not very hard. She lost her footing and fell to the deck. She hit the back of her head. I bent down and she was completely out. But she was breathing. I have no doubt about that." Maddie started crying. Rory consoled her with a hug. " I didn't know what to do! She was too tall for me to lift. So, I went back to the band quarters and told Rory."

"She did, Rory McDowell said. "It was just a matter of minutes. We went into the restroom there and discussed it. She was crying when she told me where it happened. We decided I should go down and be sure Quinn was ok. It was dark. She might not be found for a while. I did that. She was not there. I just figured she had recovered and was somewhere on board. I didn't see her, and I didn't know what to think when she didn't turn up for the show."

"What time was that?" Cragen asked.

"It was about 10 or 15 minutes past 7:00. It was very dark in that corner too. They should have a light by the restroom. They don't."

" You didn't shove her over the edge?" George stood up to give his question more attention.

" I would never do that to anyone. Quinn was one of my favorite people and a valuable asset to the band. We will all miss her!"

Cragen asked if that was all. The couple nodded in unison.

"Why didn't you report this?"

Rory sat back in his chair and said," we knew that Maddie would be suspected of killing her if we offered anything. I couldn't let that happen. Blame me for that, I guess."

"I will have to detain you both and charge you for withholding information. I would like you to completely write up as much detail as you can remember and both of you sign it. Have your attorney help you. If you are certainly not guilty of throwing her overboard, we will prove it. Don't be concerned. We will do our best! Don't leave anything out of your statement."

George and Cragen headed for the door. In the hall, Cragen stopped George. "Charge them —'withholding evidence' and read them their rights. Get that statement!"

"I will sir.

CHAPTER 23 LIFE CONTINUES ON

So, Mary Bell was officially out of work again and waiting for her new job. She held to her decision to change her life. Her and George went to the Sunday morning service at Lighthouse Christian Church and expressed to each other how they enjoyed it. They listened intently to the lesson, and Pastor Daniel made them feel welcome. They wanted to know more. He gave them both a bible and they were looking forward to studying with him in the future. Mary and George were planning their summer wedding and decided this was the place where they wanted to be married .

They continued to attend each Sunday morning . We find later that they became members one Sunday morning in 2022 as they answered the call to be baptized into Christ and enter his kingdom. They got to know the congregation and even played their instruments in the service at times. They were content!

Back to our November dates. Cragen was enjoying his time with his wife and children and with the rush over and the case at a standstill, they were all looking forward to an exciting Thanksgiving Day dinner. And their big old historic home could well accommodate the siblings coming from New York. His parents also expressed they might be able to come. It would be an exciting time for the family.

Cragen was waiting for the whole scenario to come together with the Sea Lion case.

Quinn and Jake were still in hiding. Nothing had happened there.

And I and my guest were going to take a break. She was going to her home, which was outside of town quite a bit. I would set down at the computer and put down these words on paper. I had gathered so much information. I, like the Astoria Police Department, did not know who the murderer was. But I would dwell on it. I could produce an idea of sorts. We had helped a bit.

'THE YARD DOGS'

And, the Police Department has its own band. The history of this groups extends back to 2019 county fair. The three Police Department guys are Kevin Berry, Chris McLeary and Andrew Randall (Yard Dogs band.) They came together with Jason Hoover from the Clatsop County Sheriff's Office and Keith Warren who is a Port of Astoria security office. They started as a group named 'Public Nuisance.' Their fundraiser at the fairgrounds was dedicated to 'The Oregon Fallen Badge Foundation' which helps supports the families of fallen officers. They noted that this foundation had did much for Police Sergeant Jason Goodding who was killed in the line of duty in 2016.

Covid-19 shut down so many plans and it affected this group also. So, they play according to their work schedules. Now the members of 'Yard Dogs' are getting back to public performances. George Van has decided to join them if they can stand a banjo among all those guitars.

Keith Warren(Port Security)
And Astoria Police Officers
Christopher McLeary
Kevin Berry
Andrew Randall

They would perform once in December and were also Scheduled for a New year's Eve performance.

CHAPTER 24 BACK TO THE CASE:

Astoria, Oregon is a quaint, quiet town of ten thousand people. It is hard to believe this little city could have two such murder cases within the year. I enjoyed writing up the first murder of the clown in 2021. I enjoyed talking to citizens who were quite concerned over the 'goings-on.' I am a writer after all. Astoria tourist season is very hard to deal with, and fate dealt a hand with these murders.

So, I sit with Abigail on a bench looking out on the Columbia River. We see in the distance the shore of Washington State. We see the 4-mile Astoria Bridge to Washington, and we see the cars coming and going to the shopping centers of Warrenton and to the tourist spots around our beautiful city. It is sometimes so overwhelming to us.

Abigail looks like she wants to comment. I turn to her and say, " you've got a thought, Abigail? Tell me about it. "

"Well, I'm just considering who could be responsible for this murder. They have three suspects in jail now. Do you think?"--she hesitated.

"I'm not sure. The McDowell's seemed to be quite sincere."

"And Captain Murphy? What do you think about him?"

"Time will tell. He does not seem to be too cooperative. If the CIA were after him on the oversea cruise, he could be suspicious of Quinn getting information from his buddies. They arrested some."

Abigail sighed and said "I guess you could be right. There might be something there."

I commented on her photography. "What do you think of putting many photos in the book?" I said. "I noticed you're taking more pictures than I am. You may have some good ones."

"Aw, I'm not much of a photographer, but I noted when reading your last book that photos make a difference. They seem to help the reader get more of an understanding of the story."

I agreed with Abigail on that.

She continued. "You know I would like to get pictures of the house where they are staying. How neat would that be? Do you think we could find out?"

"Abigail, I think that would be the last thing that they are going to let out. It's up to the department. We'll see. They may think it would be too dangerous for us."

"Yes, they might think that. You know, we have been quite a bit of help already, however." She shrugged her shoulders and went to another thought. " It's good I'm going home for a couple of days. I just heard I've got friends coming in from out of town. I've just got to be there. My car is parked right down the block. I'll just walk down—save you starting up your car. I do need to get home before dark. I don't drive late anymore." She got up from the bench and headed to the street.

I understood that. I was of the same   mind-set. "Have a good trip back to Scappoose, Abigail. I'll call you if anything happens."

"Please do. I can't wait to see how this story comes out." Maybe they will let you know where Quinn and her friend are staying"

"Could be. I will ask. Bye now!"

DeLores May Studying the case

I headed home also--to a big Thanksgiving dinner!

CHAPTER 25 NOVEMBER WOULD NEVER END:

It happened quicker than they thought it would. The Coast Guard recovered the FBI woman's purse from the river and turned it into the department.

Cragen and George put it up on the table and sorted through it. They found a Glock 23-40 S&W-compact model FBI issue. It was quite small, but perfect for their Astoria agent. There was the usual assemblage of women's cosmetics and her ID and driver's license. It showed that she was Sandy Hues, an FBI agent for sure. Her picture was there but it showed deep brown hair—not red.

Cragen called the front desk." Send a fingerprint expert to my office if you would. I want all the prints you can find in this purse." Cragen and George were both impressed on how well articles inside were preserved. "This is a very well-sealed bag. I'm surprised. I think, if the murderer touched any of it inside, we're gonna get prints!"

George agreed. "This could be a reliable source of clues!"

" I'm going to see what ID the prints of the body give us also. They should be in by now."

The prints were a match to the body. And this was

Miss Hue's ID in this purse

So, the Police Depart has three suspects in its custody. Maddie and Rory McDowell. She could have did it. Or--he could have did it to protect her. Or—the Captain—still a suspect might have shoved her over. And there were others out there who definitely had a motive of some kind. What about the drug dealers and the double-agent Russian spies? We will see!

And the next day I was called into the police station. It was a surprise to me. George sat at the conference table. CSI O'Neal was on his way in from his office.

They both motioned me in, and we all sat down. Cragen closed the door.

" Ms. Ruby—how well do you know her?" George spoke first.

"Well, I've known her about five years. She's been a good friend indeed. Always been there to help. I rely on her some."

CSI Cragen O'Neal leaned over the table. "Well, guess what, DeLores May? It's just policy to check out all our fingerprints whether we have suspicions or not. We checked Abigail's prints along with the others- the band, the crew, the passengers. We even checked yours! Here's what came back." Standing up he told me.

"Her name is actually Camilla Nova. She did work for that company. But she was fired and arrested for stealing file information and forwarding it to others. It was quite a scandal. She served two years in prison. She could have served more but she turned state's information and they rounded up a whole organized group of information thieves. She had been doing that for years. She is only sixty-five. She used information from a file she had stolen to change her name and so she had a whole new ID. That's when she showed up at your apartments. And she knew that the new name she had would get her good references and credit. So, of course, you would put her in an apartment."

"Why—" I was shocked and took a moment to answer. " She's always been such a good person and so helpful."

I was still trying to get a handle on this latest information that was being given to me. "Do you think she could be involved?"

George answered. "She's pretty old to do something like that. We don't think that at this time. There is no supporting evidence implicating her. We thought you would want to watch her pretty close, however. Keep her out of our office. Watch what she says and does."

"She wants to co-author with me on this book. I'm not sure I would feel good about that at all. She did say something strange before she left yesterday. She thought we should find out where Quinn and Jake were hiding so we could take photos for the book. I thought it strange. There is a limit to what you will let us do."

" That is strange." Cragen shook his head slowly. "We do appreciate how you are helping us out. And we do know you have not revealed anything to the press except what we wanted you to. You are valuable to us, DeLores May."

"Thank you. I've tried to be. My new book will be my best, I think. Abigail will not be back for a couple of days. I will keep my eyes and ears open when she returns."

Cragen continued. "We are getting breaks. This morning we got a call from a passenger who has been out of town quite a while. She found out about the murder. She said she came out of the restroom to find the lady on the floor. She couldn't lift her, so she went to the desk and reported it. They were going to help her. So, Captain Murphy might have known. She thought that the lady was ok---had too much to drink. That is interesting too. It gives credence to Maddie McDowell's story. Whatever happened to our FBI agent happened quickly—in an instant. There were too many people coming and going. And that puts Captain Murphy on the scene --a suspect. If he thought Quinn knew about his drug dealing, he would do it, wouldn't he?"

I left the police station with mixed emotions. Abigail had been such a friend to me, I could hardly believe this. But it was true. She was a criminal. I would have to approach this very carefully. I went to the KD

Properties office where I found Sherry hard at work on the accounts. She was so good on research.

"Sherry, we have a situation. The lady that rented from us—Abigail Ruby—she was not who we thought she was. Her real name was Camilla Nova. She has served time in prison. This will be confidential. Don't tell anyone. Can you research her name?"

"I'm so sorry, mom! I know she's a good friend and means so much to you. You need lady friends even if you are so close to Dad. We all do, I think." She paused at her computer. "I can go through a name search. I know we don't usually do that but, in this case, I think we should."

"If this helps solve this case by adding a bit of information, it's worth it." I said.

When I left the office, I was sure Sherry could find all we needed.

I would spend a couple of days at home-writing down all my findings up to now. How was this case going to come together? I know Officers Cragen and George are being careful about filling me in on facts now. They must have more information. I know that.

CHAPTER 26 CLOSE FRIEND?

I'm going to plead busy at home when Abigail comes back. I can't take a chance that she has anything to do with the case. The police may think she's too old to be involved, but I know at 86, I'm quite active. I spent the next day or so writing down what I knew. I can always go back and correct pages when I have more information. Then I called the station. I told George that I had Abigail's address in Scappoose, and that I was going to just quickly visit her. I had never been there. George said they would appreciate that, but don't get into any situations. I told him I would be careful as 'a beaver cutting his next tree down.' He laughed!

I told Ken what I was going to do. He let me know he was going to drive. He would come along. I felt better about that. "You are getting so involved with this case. I'm not sure it's a good idea." Ken knew he couldn't change my mind, but he would certainly make sure I was safe.

I have a sister in Scappoose so I would have an excuse for visiting. Her name is June.

We stopped at her house for a few minutes. June was glad to see us. She was by herself since she lost her husband a number of years ago and had recently also had problems with her health. She was feeling good. Her grandkids lived nearby and her husband's daughter.

She told me all about them and their plans for the holidays. It would include family. And she was also beginning to go back to bowling and golf. She was always active and walked miles per day. A small heart attack didn't keep her down.

I told her about the case being careful not to reveal much about Abigail. Scappoose was a small town. Did she know Abigail?

"Yes, she's in my book club. Right now, we are reading your book, 'My Great Grandfather's Poems.' She was so interested. She said she knew you."

"You know, she didn't say anything to me about knowing my sis. I'm surprised!"

June stood up and said, "Abigail fits into Scappoose well. I see her all over town doing this and that. Masks don't keep us from getting out."

" I admire your activity. It's not everyone who has had a heart attack that will do what you do."

June fixed us a lite lunch. We said our goodbyes. I invited her to visit us.

As we walked to her door, June said, "You know that my new car makes a difference in me being able to drive more. I will plan the next trip to Astoria."

Scappoose is small town. Abigail lived in a nice housing development. The homes were expensive.

Her house was large. It looked like it had a swimming pool (enclosed)-- more luxuries than I thought she could pay for on a small pension. With the increase of Portland workers buying in Scappoose, because of this town's short distance from Portland, real estate was increasing in value. Ken and I figured this house value would be at least $750,000 or more. We know June's house was over half a mil.

We rang. Abigail answered the door.

She seemed ill at ease at first, then quickly brightened up and invited us into her foyer. I told her that I had visited my sister and while in the neighborhood I wanted to drop by. We walked into the luscious living room with soaring ceilings and hardwood floors throughout. We looked across the room to see the huge kitchen with granite cabinet tops. There was natural wood everywhere. Setting in a side room was a beautiful maple grand piano finished elaborately with curls and fancy design throughout. I was impressed. It looked like Abigail had picked a permanent house and was not going anywhere. She had money. Why was I buying her all those lunches?

Ken and I sat down on her living room plush sofa. There across the room were two young men dressed in business suits—in their thirties or forty's.

"Oh, this must be your company that you were expecting."

The men stood up to be introduced.

"Yes, this is Gilbert (Call him Gil) and John Bradley. This is my good friend from Astoria, DeLores May Richards and her husband, Ken."

Abigail took a chair, and everyone followed at her nod.

"Gil and John worked at my company for five years. I was so happy to see them."

"Likewise, we are glad to be here with you, Ma'am." John leaned back in the recliner. "We had to stop for a visit. We are vacationing. Abigail told us she would take us around the coast area, and we are happy to take her up on that offer. We didn't expect that!"

"Well, you guys are going to have to change to beach clothes, I think. The coast is sand up to your ears," Ken commented.

John said, "We will, we want to get out of these flight clothes for sure. We haven't been here long. And it can wear you out on a long flight when you have to wear masks. We'll take the day to settle in and head down to Astoria tomorrow."

Gil said that he had been wanting to come to the Oregon coast for a long time. " I'm excited!"

Abigail expressed her thoughts "You know I have not even did a sightseeing tour myself. All those wonderful places you are mentioning in your books —I'm anxious to see them. I've only seen the museum."

"I'll make sure you have a complete list." I glanced down at my phone. "I have a text message. Excuse me for a bit." I walked to the kitchen and leaned on the countertop, pointed my camera at the guys and got a few photos. They were talking back and forth with Ken and didn't notice. 'Good shots,' I said to myself. I was suspicious. Why does she still have contact with them if she betrayed the company? That didn't make sense.

I walked back into the living room area and sat down. "That was Sergeant George Van. Him and CSI O'Neal has considered our request to see the house where the CIAs are. They are thinking up a good plan where we can be of help."

"Oh, well, comes at an inconvenient time. I'm going to be on a fun vacation tour. I would like—"

Gil interrupted." No, Abigail, you should go if DeLores needs you. John and I can keep ourselves busy for the morning hours for sure. I hear going to the museum will take most of the day."

"Well, DeLores May, I can spend part of a day with you. And these guys would like a little time away from 'grandma! Just let me know when you find out something."

I gave her a hug and we left. As we got into our car, I said to Ken, " Fraid I didn't get that text from George. I was taking pictures. Something seems wrong."

He said, "You are going to have to be careful, Love.

Even if she's not involved, you're dealing with real criminals. I worry about you."

"I know you do. But we have been a tremendous help. I'll be careful. Sergeant George will not let me do anything dangerous."

And that was it. I dropped Ken off at home and headed back to the department.

CHAPTER 27 SORTING OUT MATTERS:

George and Cragen were together in the coffee room when I got there. I was asked to wait in the conference room and Officer Kay would let them know I was here. It was five minutes, and they came in with steaming hot coffee and a cup for me.

They set down. I was excited about my findings. "I did get down to Scappoose with Ken this morning. I wanted to catch you before you headed for home. I visited Abigail's home. She has a very expensive house. She had her out-of-town guests there—two young guys-30's or 40's---that age group. She said that she had worked with them at her former company."

"Whoa, slow down, DeLores May. You are wound up. Let's go over this. "George had barely sat down.

" I have a sister there in Scappoose. It was a good excuse."

"And these guests were younger?'

"They Seemed like an odd match," I said.

"That does seem so!" Cragen added.

" I took pictures of them- they didn't look like tourists—business suits and all. "I   pretended like I was getting a text. It was easy to get their pictures. I did tell Abigail you might be able to let us know where the house is. I hope I didn't go overboard."

"We have been waiting for some kind of opportunity for another leak to move this along," Cragen said. "What can we do, George?"

George rubbed his palms together. "We need a plan —but we don't want to put you at risk, DeLores May. That's not what we do. How about letting her know a fake address first thing in the morning."

Cragen agreed "We could have men in place. You should say that you had something really important to do and couldn't go over there and ask her to take pictures for the book. If she's innocent, she'll take pictures only. If she's not, she will do something that will make us suspicious. Text these photos to us and we'll work over here in the office and see who they are—text their names too if you would. We will check them out first thing in the morning ."

"If these guys are spies, we had better have a lot of guys hidden out in the house." George expressed concern.

"Here is Abigail's info. She was convicted in 2010 —spent two years in jail. Then she dropped off the radar. When did she rent from you?"

I searched my memory. " I think about 2015—for five years. She was at Riverview Terrace. I'll check with Sherry."

"So, we don't know where she was between 2012

and 2015—that's three years." George emphasized the three. Cragen said, "Let's take a look at these pictures and go back to that video and do some more research. This added info might help."

"Yes, I'm willing to stay over, sir."

"However, "I can't allow you to go there tomorrow, DeLores May, as we would have to put in extra guards to protect you. And we really don't have extra people to spare for very long."

I stopped at the apartment office for a quick visit. Sherry had found that Abigail was in New York at that time. Her call for references all verified that. So, the name change must have been right after her prison term. I called George and let him know Abigail's previous address. Then, the next morning, I talked to Abigail on my cell phone and gave her the decoy address. She said she would take those pictures for me—first thing."

CHAPTER 28 MORE SUPECTS--MORE WORK:

The police department of Astoria did find themselves rushed to get all the new evidence in. The two young men were actually the two spies that the FBI was looking for. They obtained their prints from back east and searched the prints from the boat. They came up with no matches. Abigail had already left her home so they had no idea where to find them; they would have to wait. They reran the security video in case they were wearing gloves—nothing. In viewing, they found that Abigail was on the plank coming in about fifteen minutes before the boat left on the night of the murder. Before they had not had contact with Abigail Ruby. They couldn't have recognized her when they looked at the video the first time.

The FBI informed their agents that the decoy address had been passed on. They were on the alert. Abigail was given an address on Young's River Road—across from the old bridge. The house stood by itself facing an empty pasture. If there was a shootout, there was no way that bystanders could get hurt. Quinn and Jake were still at the house on Franklin Street.

CSI Cragen had matched the dent on the FBI agent's head to the floor of the boat. This particular location had small, indented circles on that part of the deck.

She showed up at the house by herself. She got out of her SUV and took out her cell phone. Abigail pointed it directly at Saddleback Mountain which was off in the distance. Then, cautiously turning the phone, she took a photo of pasture, house and anything else that might be available that might spike the guys' interest. They were not with her. She smiled as she got back into her car. What a convenient location!

The beautiful Saddleback Mountain

A couple of officers followed her. They had no success in finding her friends as she never made physical contact.

CSI Cragen looked over the evidence so far. George was in Cragen's office sorting through the paperwork.

"George, have Officer Kay get this into some kind of order. So, we put these three up on the board with the other suspects. Now we have how many?"

"Well, sir, we have these three, four in the band, the captain and the crew members. Leave those two spies up there. If they didn't push her over, they could still be involved with Abigail—I count close to ten—could be more. It may be a group effort—quite possibly. Time will tell!"

(The river walk where we exercised)

CHAPTER 29 SOMETHING SURPRISING:

It wasn't something that we expected. December had been a slow month and the beginning to 2022 was coming quickly. This month was always slow it seemed. Family activities took up the time. Ken and I had begun a morning ritual—a riverwalk. We had gotten to the sea lion area. We looked over at our unwelcome guests. "They are staying longer every year. There are a number that are now full-time residents." I said.

Ken followed the direction of my pointing finger. His long-distance eyes were terrific. Often, he had showed me things that had not been visible at first to my eyes. We enjoyed the view of the river with its turns and twists. And there the lions were—just a few. He said. "Hon, look there—the police cars up on the highway!"

I looked. Those remaining Sea Lions were being upset with the police cars flashing their lights—especially during their early morning sleep time. 'What's happening?" I said.

"That's a body that they are pulling out of the water—definitely." We hurried along and took a short cut around the blockade. We could see clearly now. Sergeant George was standing on the bank supervising.

"Abigail! Oh no!"

George called us over. "Execution style-a bullet right through the middle of the temple." He sighed.

"What--?" I muttered.

"Looks like she was no longer any use to them. Abigail would have turned state's evidence again, I'm sure. They knew her well. They were through with her."

"Yes, she would have. I have learned so much about my friend this last week. This is so sad!"

George walked back to water's edge" She never could get away from her true nature, could she?"

I turned away, brushing a tear out of my eye. Ken was there. He lent a shoulder for support

"Stop over at the office later, DeLores May. I need you to sign paperwork identifying her. We will go after those guys. We will get them."

I nodded. I would. And the Astoria Police Department would do their work!

As we went back on the riverwalk path to find our car, I could not keep the tears from flowing. Remembering the good times we had together—the friend indeed she was--the enjoyment she had reading and discussing my books. She was always ready to drop her knitting needles for an adventure to the museum or an exploration to the beach. "I didn't know her, did I, hon?"

"No, I'm afraid you didn't."

That day was one of the saddest days for me. I can see now why I should have listened to his warning about being too involved with the case. I could have easily been hurt in the crossfires. No more sleuthing for me. I'm through with that!

Back to the Sea Lions which was where it all started.

Back to the feller with his loud noisy bark.

We find a new body—it's in the water!

The Lions are there as they were before.

This body is different. I know her quite well.

She is looking up at me—my friend Abigail!

CHAPTER 30 THE END AT LAST:

The case ended abruptly. The face recognition software showed the two men to be the spies that were on the loose. The spies did not know the police department had the decoy house stocked with officers. The other house across from it had FBI agents which had been flown in.

The two spies had called their friends in to help them to take out Jake and Quinn. They thought six more would be enough, but they didn't count on 2 dozen excellent sharpshooters as opponents. The moment they crept around the side of the house to break into the back, they were surrounded with no place to run. It was an easy catch. As they were handcuffed, Astoria police cars with sirens blasting showed up from unknown locations. And the noise hardly woke the neighbors because of the country location.

The FBI took them into immediate custody and headed to their private plane at the Portland airport.

The next morning, I stopped early at the police department to ID the body. I had pretty well gotten over my negative attitude and was ready to finish my book. Sergeant George was in O'Neal's office having coffee.

"DeLores May," he called out. "We're in here."

I walked into the office. George and Cragen were finishing paperwork on the case and were anxious to share. George spoke first. "We got them—about midnight last night."

"Oh, I am so glad." I said as I sat down.

Cragen said, "yes, and without a shot. We had them outnumbered. They didn't have a chance!" He was elated. "The FBI took them right away. So, we are through with them completely. We didn't even have to be there—just sleeping away till they called."

George said, "They were definitely the two spies the FBI was looking for."

"Well." I said. Were they the ones who killed Abigail?"

George answered. "They haven't admitted it yet, but we think the FBI will be finding that to be a fact shortly."

"Poor Abigail!"

Cragen was quick to relate. "Don't feel sorry for her, Ma'am. We have found out things about Abigail Ruby. When she left prison and changed her name, she ended up being an assassin for the spy gang. Those years she spent in New York?--that's what she was doing. She would just as soon murder as look at a person twice. That's where she got all her money."

"Oh-how-how could she do that?"

"Simple, it was her nature. She liked her work and who would suspect a little old, retired lady? Her bank account was worth millions."

"And finally, she took those millions and got as far away as she could from the east coast—and retired. That's where you came in. She bought that lovely home in Scappoose, but she also rented from your company just to have a place on the coast."

"And I felt sorry for her and made her my friend. She had no family. I know better than to make tenants friends too. I did it, anyway, didn't I?" I was speaking to myself.

Cragen looked over at me. "Don't feel bad. We were taken in too. They found out where she was and offered her a high price to kill Quinn. She couldn't refuse for that much. Her close association with you was to obtain information. As it stands now, we think she pushed the FBI agent off the boat deck because she thought she was Quinn. The purse that the Coast Guard found was so dry inside. Her prints were on the ID. She pushed the poor lady over the edge and left quickly for another part of the boat. By the time the Captain got there and Maddie's husband also, the deed had been done. She found later that she killed the wrong woman. The purse went into the river."

George said " We learned a lesson. No more putting little 86-year-old ladies at risk. Don't expect it, DeLores May! But we do thank you for your help regardless. We got the bad guys, didn't we?"

"You can say that for sure." I shook hands with the officers, turned and walked out to the street.

I think I will have a walk and we will visit the museum.

This is the 'Bowpicker.' It's a good place for fish and chips and right across from both museums.

UPPER TOWN

As we approach upper town's Museum, we find that we can spend the day looking at all the River attractions—and all right there steps away.

This museum has a reference library of over 20,000 journals and manuscripts, 30,000 historic photos, and 1,000 charts and maps. If you are interested in maritime history, this is the place to go!

THE HERITAGE MUSEUM

Walk across Marine drive and walk up the hill and you will come across the Heritage Museum. It was completed in 1905 as the Astoria City Hall—once the police station and jail in the basement, police court and city offices on the first floor and the public library and council chambers on the second floor. In 1941 the USO used it to house workers because of the World War II boom. After the USO put the building to leisure space, they continued their use thru the 1961 closure of the Naval base.

Then in 1962 the Columbia River Maritime Museum opened and stayed there for 20 years until they opened in their current location.

In 1982, the Clatsop County Historical Society became the primary source to tell the story of the history of Astoria and Clatsop County.

You can look across the parking and see the old brick Railroad station. It was built in 1924 to replace the old wooden depot that was built in the 1890's. This brick building's exterior was restored in 2002 for the Lewis Clark explorer passenger trains (2002-2005.) The inside of the station is not available to see.

The history of the railroad itself is long and involved. Ever since Astoria was founded in 1811, residents wanted their town to become a booming port. Years passed before they completed their railroad. In 1898 it was done with the work of Andrew B. Hammond from Montana. But, although the Astorian wanted a port for business, it proved to be more of a tourist use for Portlanders wanting to come to the coast and escape Portland heat. That was the beginning of what Astoria is now known for--tourism. The timber industry benefited mostly from the ARC railroad aside from the tourist industry, however. Access was now available for moving timber products without being concerned about the mountains and valleys. The line was abandoned in the 1990's. You still see the tracks parallel to the Riverwalk, and they are usable in Astoria proper for the local trolley which has been a tourist attraction in the summer.

'THE PILOT BOAT PEACOCK'
THIS TUGBOAT IS WITHIN FEET OF
THE MARITIME MUSEUM. IT WAS
DECOMMISSIONED IN 1999. THE PEACOCK
CROSSED THE COLUMBIA RIVER BAR MORE
THAN 35,000 TIMES DURING ITS THIRTY
PLUS YEAR CAREER. BUILT IN GERMANY
AND DELIVERED FOR SERVICE IN 1967, SHE
IS NINETY FEET LONG AND THIRTY-THREE
FEET TALL. A DAUGHTER BOAT TWENTY-
THREE FEET LONG HINGED TO THE STERN
WAS USED IN HARSH WEATHER TO DO THE
ACTUAL TRANSFER OF PILOTS BETWEEN
SHIP AND PILOT BOAT. HER TOP SPEED
WAS TWENTY-THREE MPH. SHE CARRIED
A CREW OF THREE AND UP TO TWELVE
PILOTS.

SWENSON BLACKSMITH SHOP

Courtesy of Wikipedia)

Built in 1920, this is a photo of the Swenson Blacksmith shop taken in 2010. It is located at 1769 Exchange Street. Walk or Drive by to see history. Note the historic details.

"AMERICAN EXPRESS RIVER CRUISE"

This River Cruise goes up and down the Columbia River. It's a spendy trip. But the guests love it. They have roomy state rooms. They visit towns. They stay in deluxe hotels. They have three big greyhound-size buses to take them around the area. They dock close to the museum, also.

A CRUISE SHIP DOCKED

In October 2020, the port of Astoria played host to the MS Regatta for a total of $75,000 per month. It's date of departure was to be April 2021.The business of docking cruise ships has helped with the loss of business from the lack of cruise landings in Astoria during the pandemic.

The American Pride also docked for a period of 6 months at a very profitable fee for the port. The picture above was taken in November of a cruise ship docked in the river close to the museum.

THE RIVERWALK

This trail follows the city's waterfront and along a portion of the Astoria and Columbia River Railroad. It's 12.8 miles long with views of the Columbia , Youngs Bay, and the impressive Astoria-Megler Bridge. You will come across the museum sites that are listed above and more!

Here you see the Trolley on the Riverwalk

Run by volunteers, Old 300 was built in 1913. It was part of the San Antonio Public Service Co. This ended in 1933. It was brought to Astoria, restored by volunteers in 1998. Tours start March 25th and run through October 30. The website advertises rides for

$1 or $2 for all day. You can see the Columbia River and historic sites.

And beyond the city the Riverwalk extends to Tongue point. In March of 1806, the Lewis and Clark Expedition camped here after wintering at Fort Clatsop. Clark named it 'Point William.' A worthwhile tourist attraction is the Lewis Clark National Historic Trail. Its use today is a U.S. Job Corps Campus, US Coast Guard Facility, commercial shipping yards, and a national wildlife refuge.

And we end up where we began at 'The Rogue Ale Public House.' Don't forget to visit the Bumble Bee free museum at Rogue Ale also. It's lunchtime at this fine restaurant. And I am having chowder and 'Deadman's fish and chips.'

Bumble Bee free museum located at The Rogue Ale.
A walk through is recommended.

COLUMBIA RIVER

Viewing our mighty Columbia river from
the deck of the Rouge Ale Public House

AN APPROPRIATE END

The Columbia River looking over to the hills
of Washington state on a sunny day

EPILOGUE 2021 ENDS IN ASTORIA :

In 2022, the end of the pandemic brings a new freedom to the streets of Astoria. The Astoria/ Warrenton Crab Seafood and Wine Festival is scheduled for April and The Tenor guitar gathering for June. The rest of the summer activities will no doubt follow with in their respective months. There are now only twenty-one—cut in half-- cruise ships coming into port in 2022. Astoria is a good place to be.

Your soon to be 87-year-old author has decided, after her experience with crime fighting that she will stick with book writing.

Mary Bell: January will begin her career started as emergency dispatch operator, but since all cities are now temporarily combined, is she too far away from the Astoria office? The office is in Seaside. So, what about Mary Bell and Sergeant George Van? Do they decide to go ahead with marriage plans or does this barrier make them change their minds? And what about their music?

Does CSI O'Neal continue as lead detective and Forensic medical examiner or is it too much for him?

WHAT HAPPENS TO CIA AGENTS QUINN AND JAKE?

The reader will discover the surprising rating that Oregon has in Drug and Alcohol addiction. And what they are doing about it! Does this effect the sudden incidents of murders that we see in the community?

And Portland will decide that they need to send a couple of lady detective sleuths to temporarily help out Astoria police. But—is this helping? Or does the clumsiness of these two ladies add to the confusion? Does Portland just want to get rid of them?

Come to Astoria in 2022. Join the
great continuing adventure.

IN MEMORY OF ASTORIA POLICE OFFICERS

SAM WHISLER (2021)

JASON GOODDING (2016)

BOOKS BY THIS AUTHOR

Astoria Mysteries -Gulley's Butcher Shop-The Clown

The first book in the Astoria Mysteries series is a tale about a dead clown in Gulley's Butcher shop in Astoria, Ore. The butcher shop is real and the owners are real people. Officer George Van and CSI Cragen O'Neal are the fiction murder solvers in this series. You will wonder what is real and what is fiction!

Astoria Mysteries-Sea Lion Scenario

This second book follows A beautiful red-headed lady is found deceased among the Astoria sea lions. Twists and turns are in the works as the officers solve this strange murder. The author puts herself into this story to help in solving this crime.

All these books are available at Amazon.com

BOOKS BY THIS AUTHOR

Music From My Heart Volume One And Two

The first book contains the authors original songs from 1955 to 2020. It includes family photos and history. The second book is a presentation of her current melodies.

My Great Grandfather's Poems Volume One And Two. And Book Three Will Be Available In August Of 2022

Daniel Franklin Howard lived from 1841-1837. He published a book: "Oregon's first white men." He wrote historical poems all through his life including his service in the civil war. He wished someday that they would be published. The author is presenting her great Grandfather's poems with history and comments.

Made in the USA
Columbia, SC
19 September 2022